Washed Away

Doug Fletcher book 2

Dean L. Hovey

Print ISBNs

LSI Print 9780228609773

BWL Publishing Inc.

Books we love to write ...
Authors around the world.

http://bwlpublishing.ca

To Charity, Heather, and Garret
I'd like to acknowledge and thank

BWL Publishing, Renee Duke, and Jude Pittman

Julie, my wife, for putting up with my endless hours on the computer

Lois Johnson for proofreading and her ongoing support

Anne Flagge for her proofreading, suggestions and continuous support

Natalie Lund for decades of support, suggestions, critique, and proofreading

Mike Westfall for his assistance with the technical details of desert hiking and camping

Frannie Brozo who read an early draft of *Stolen Past* and asked, "What's the plot of the next Doug Fletcher book?"

Dan Fouts and Larry Hawes for reading early drafts offering opinions and support

Chapter 1

Elizabeth "Liz" Carpenter had been a Park Service ranger and backcountry guide for three years. She'd endured withering heat, heavy snow, drunks, unprepared neophytes, and condescending jerks. She was as capable as any of her male counterparts. She wore her short brown hair under a bandana that doubled as a sweatband. After three years of hiking trails carrying a fifty-pound backpack, she was built more like an athlete than a ballerina. In addition to her personal camping supplies she carried a butane stove, an aluminum cook kit (pot, frying pan, plates, cups), dehydrated food, four gallons of water, extra "space" blankets, toilet paper, garbage bags, hand sanitizer, a first aid kit, a folding hunting knife, a folding shovel, and a cellphone.

Liz had developed her own one-to-ten rating system for hiking groups. Looking over this group at the trailhead, she'd rated them a six. The three generations of a family consisted of two grandparents, two parents, and three grandchildren. They weren't backcountry hikers, but they arrived with well-worn backpacks for their overnight hike including tents, blankets, a gallon of water each, dried food, and granola bars. The grandparents and parents wore scarred hiking boots and two layers of socks. Liz knew they wouldn't be suffering from blisters. Two of the grandchildren were teen girls, Courtney, 17, and Ann, 16. They weren't as well prepared as their parents and grandparents, wearing fashionably tattered jeans and athletic shoes, but they would make up for their lack of hiking experience by being young, in shape, and energetic. The third grandchild, Mike, was a problem; he was barely over the minimum age requirement for the backcountry trek the family had drawn in a lottery.

Mike wore scarred tennis shoes without laces and exuded "attitude." He argued every suggestion and ran ahead or lagged behind. At least a third of the time Mike was out of sight, causing Liz to jog ahead or backtrack to return him to the group. He was the reason she hadn't rated the group a seven at the beginning of the hike. Because of Mike, their rating was rapidly slipping toward four.

The grandparents moved along at a moderate pace, stopping only to take pictures of the petroglyphs and scenery. The family was pleasant, inquisitive, and appreciative of the natural history Liz provided. The October morning was cool when they departed. The temperature had risen steadily, moderated by the nearly six-thousand-foot altitude. With the sun near its apex, the temperature climbed into the eighties. Liz reminded them to drink to stay hydrated, saying even though their shirts weren't wet, they were sweating. The dry high desert air wicked away moisture as fast as it formed. Thunder rumbled in the distance—a late 'monsoon season' storm was dropping rain somewhere north of them even though the sky above them was blue.

Three hours into the hike they arrived at the ultimate photo opportunity, a canyon eroded from the layered sedimentary rock by water and wind. The twisting canyon turns were irregularly cut into the stone. They paused in two spots to take pictures. Mike never stopped moving. Uninterested in the natural history or scenery, he roved ahead of the group as the others took photos, awed by the natural beauty.

The mother's patience had worn through. "Michael! Get back here!" She gave Liz a pleading look.

Liz nodded, and jogged ahead. It took her nearly five minutes to find Mike, who was scratching at the canyon wall with a rock, apparently trying to carve his initials into the stone. Liz was reasonably certain she was out of the family's hearing.

"You little shit." Mike, unfazed by her profanity, kept scratching at the sandstone. Liz approached him and swatted

7

the small stone from his hand. "Take only pictures and leave only footprints."

Mike gave her a withering glare. "Fuck off." He stood up and brushed the dust from his denim shorts.

Liz grabbed the loop on his backpack and lifted him until only his toes were touching the ground. "You can get by with that around your parents, but I don't have to take any of your shit. You either join the group and act like a human being or I'm going to grab your collar and drag you back every time you're a step ahead or behind."

Mike gave her a look of disdain. In return, she shook his collar and lifted him entirely off the ground. "Do you understand me?"

"I'm going to tell my mom about this and you're not going to get a tip."

"The joke's on you. Rangers can't accept tips." Liz lowered Mike to the ground. "She might donate a hundred bucks to the park if I can make you behave like an adult."

Mike shook himself and pulled his shirt down. "All I have to do is tell her you grabbed my crotch, and you'll be lucky if you don't go to jail." He took two steps down the trail, going farther ahead of his family.

Liz grabbed his backpack. "I'm not here to be your babysitter, I'm here for your safety. We're going back to your family."

Mike swatted at her hand, but Liz pulled him backwards and started walking back toward the rest of the group. He took a few backward steps, then fell on his butt. Liz released her grip and waited for him to stand up.

"I didn't want to go on this fucked up hike. Mom took away my phone, iPad, and headphones, then told me to get into the minivan. I'm done."

"Get up."

"No. I told you, I'm done walking. You can leave me alone, or carry me, but I'm not *hiking* with the family anymore."

"Fine. Sit here until your mother catches up, then you're her problem." When Mike made no move, Liz started back toward the rest of the family. She found them slowly walking toward her, three minutes behind Mike.

The father looked behind her as she approached. "Where's Michael?"

"He's staging a sit-in. I stopped him from carving his initials in the stone wall, and now he's unhappy and unwilling to walk."

Grandma clenched her teeth and glared at the mother. "He's out of control. You need to do something with him."

"He's having a bad day."

"He's a spoiled brat. If you don't deal with his behavior now, it's only going to get worse."

Mike's sisters were smiling as thunder rumbled again.

Liz looked at the sky and steep canyon walls nervously. "We sometimes get flash floods and this canyon can become a river, so you need to get to a higher elevation. Go back until you get to the gently sloping edges where you can gain some altitude. I'll get Mike and meet you on the top."

Liz jogged ahead until she found Mike scratching at the wall with a rock, his backpack laying on the ground. "C'mon. We're getting out of here."

"I'm not going anywhere with you." Mike didn't look up from his scratching.

"Did you hear the thunder? There could be a flash flood."

Mike shrugged as he continued scratching. When she reached him, she could see the "M" he'd scratched into the wall. He was starting on the "I" when she grabbed his collar and belt. In one fluid motion she lifted him and threw him toward the trail. He landed scraping his hands and knees on the loose gravel. When he stood, she saw the blood starting to seep from his skinned knees. Liz threw the backpack at him.

Mike gave Liz a withering glare. "You're fucking dead when we get back to my mom." He started marching down the trail. Liz fell in behind him wishing he would walk faster. She hoped the rest of the family had followed her directions.

Three minutes later Liz felt more than heard the rumbling. "Run!" She looked over her shoulder after a few steps. Mike plodded along, staring at the ground, and almost dragging his backpack. She jogged back to Mike and considered throwing him over her shoulder when she saw the ground behind them had turned into a mud flow. She grabbed his arm and pulled him toward a cut in the canyon wall. He tried to pull free, but she yanked him along as the mud got closer and became watery.

His backpack slipped from his hand and he stopped to pick it up.

"Leave it!"

By the time they reached the cut in the wall, the mud was at their feet. Liz glanced back and saw the flowing mud carrying Mike's backpack along with sticks and other debris as it rushed toward them. She pushed Mike up the notch in the wall, trying to find handholds in the steep rock.

Mike turned back to berate her but saw the mud rushing past below them. His eyes grew wide as it inched farther up the wall with each passing second. Young and nimble, Mike scrambled up the wall. He lost his foothold and kicked Liz's hand, causing her to slide down the steep slope, scraping her knees, chest, face, and hands. Her legs were thigh-deep in the torrent before she grabbed an outcropping. Using both hands on the rock she held on, trying to find a purchase for her feet, now under the muddy flow. The current tugged at her legs and swung them to the side until her fingers could hardly hold any longer. Kicking against the slope, her right foot found a crack and stopped her slide. Her left foot slid along the rock surface until it too found the crack. With her feet braced in the muddy slurry, she found new handholds that allowed her to pull herself up. Slowly, she inched farther and farther up the slope until she was finally out of the mucky flow. She stopped there for a few seconds, alternately shaking her arms and legs, trying to loosen them and circulate the lactic acid causing them to ache. She took a deep breath and crawled up the incline.

Liz was halfway up the notch when Mike climbed onto the mesa above. "Hurry!"

Her fingers and knees were scraped and bloody, her uniform torn and plastered to her with sweat and mud. She pulled herself to the top, collapsing and gasping for air as adrenaline coursed through her system. She lay flat on her stomach for a few seconds, then sat next to Mike and slid off the heavy backpack, catching her breath and watching the muddy torrent below them turn into a gushing river. A large dead branch washed past below them, pushed down from somewhere farther up the canyon.

Mike watched the muddy water below as Liz tried to catch her breath. "Where'd this water come from?"

"The storms north of us must've dumped several inches of rain in just a few minutes. That all collects in the arroyos before they all funnel into the canyon."

Mike looked around. "Where's my mom?"

"I don't know. I sent them down the canyon, then I went to find you."

The weight of Liz's words struck Mike. "You mean they might still be in the canyon?"

Liz stood up and looked around. They were on the mesa surrounding the canyon. It seemed like she could see for miles, but she knew the undulating land hid many of its features until you were nearly on top of them. No one was in sight. She picked up her backpack and slung it on her shoulders.

"C'mon. We'll walk back to them."

"I lost my shoes." Mike looked at his muddy socks.

Liz rolled her eyes, reflecting on the stupidity of going on a hike without shoelaces. "Watch where you step. There are little cacti all over here."

Mike fell into step beside her. "I don't see Mom or Dad."

"They're farther down the canyon."

"I don't think Grandpa can climb up a wall like we did." Mike showed the first sign of concern about anyone else since they'd started the hike.

"There are spots where the walls aren't as steep."

"Slow down!" Mike stumbled along behind Liz, who didn't break stride.

They crested a rise and saw Ann and Courtney standing with their father. All three were staring down the canyon, their backpacks nowhere in sight. They didn't notice Liz until she was beside them. They were covered with mud to mid-calf and were caked with dust over the rest of their bodies.

Liz looked the direction they were staring. "Where are the rest?"

The dad looked at her with glazed eyes. He pointed down the canyon.

Ann pointed toward a spot below them. "Grandma got caught in the mud down there. Mom and Grandpa tried to grab her, but she got sucked away."

Liz pulled the cellphone from her backpack and turned it on. After going through the start up she had one bar of service. She punched in 911. The ringing cut in and out and Liz had low expectations of being able to actually have a conversation.

"This is Coconino County dispatch. What's your emergency?"

"I'm guiding a group of hikers and we were caught in a flash flood. Three of my party are missing. We're on the Crack in the Rock trail."

"Is that in Wupatki National Monument?"

"Yes. We're about three hours up the trail."

The dispatcher's voice cut in and out. "I'll notify the Park Service. Please give me your name."

"My name is Elizabeth Carpenter. I'm a Park Service Ranger."

After a pause that made Liz think the call had been dropped, the dispatcher came back. "I've notified both Coconino County Rescue and the Park Service."

Liz shut down her phone and tucked it into the backpack. The father looked at her expectantly. "Have they been found?"

"The dispatcher didn't say."

He was in shock and obviously unable to process what had happened. "What do we do now?"

"We walk."

Chapter 2

Park Service Superintendent Jill Rickowski was talking to a group of tourists in the Sunset Crater visitor center when a seasonal ranger waved to her from behind the counter. The ranger held up a phone and pointed at her.

"Excuse me. Duty calls."

The seasonal ranger handed Jill the phone. "It's Coconino County EMS."

"This is Superintendent Rickowski."

"We received a call from one of your rangers who's guiding hikers. They've been caught in a flash flood and some of her party are missing."

Jill closed her eyes and braced herself against the counter. "Who called?"

"Elizabeth Carpenter. We've dispatched the county rescue squad. Where would you like to meet them?"

"I'll meet them at the Wupatki National Monument visitor center. Thank you."

Chapter 3

The rescue team met Liz and the family walking slowly toward the trailhead. After Liz explained what she'd done and seen, Ann told Jill, who was leading the rescue crew, about her grandparents and mother. The father continued to look dazed. Jill told a seasonal ranger to lead the family back to the visitor center.

Jill took Liz aside. "Do you know what happened to the mother and grandparents?"

Liz shook her head. "The grandson and I climbed out, then found the father and girls farther down the canyon. One of the girls said they lost track of her mom and grandparents."

Jill nodded. "It sounds like you did all the right things."

Liz, the adrenaline burning out of her system and the pressure off, started to shake. She dropped her backpack as tears ran down her cheeks. "I lost three hikers." She hugged Jill and buried her face in the superintendent's shoulder.

"They're searching. Maybe it'll turn out okay."

"It was muddy and full of sticks. They never had a chance." Jill didn't argue the point.

The portable radio on Jill's belt made a staticky announcement. Jill turned up the volume. "Please repeat."

"Jill, this is Brad Peck. I'm walking with the Coconino County rescue squad. We've found two bodies."

"No sign of the third victim?" Liz stood close beside her, listening, and biting the inside of her right cheek.

"Nothing yet."

Jill put the radio back in its holster. Liz was caked with mud and dust, with bloody scabs on her hands and knees. Her uniform blouse was missing several buttons and her badge hung from a scrap of fabric.

Jill put her hands on Liz's shoulders and looked her in the eye. "Go to your trailer, take a shower, and change into a fresh uniform. Okay?"

Liz nodded and looked around the trailhead, trying to figure out how to get back to the Park Service trailer she shared with two other female rangers. Jill threw her a key ring. "Take my truck. I'll catch a ride."

Liz was driving away when Jill responded to her name being called on the radio. "This is Brad. We have two more bodies."

"Please repeat."

"We've recovered two more bodies."

"I don't think I understood you. You have a total of two bodies, correct, Brad?"

"We have a total of four bodies."

Jill's mind raced. Was there another hiker signed in to hike the trail? Maybe someone didn't sign in and went for an illegal day hike. She scanned the vehicles in the trailhead parking lot and could account for each of them.

What the hell is going on?

Chapter 4

The last day of training at the Federal Law Enforcement Training Center (FLETC) was little more than a formality. I ate breakfast with a couple of the instructors in the cafeteria (I was the oldest person in the class and had more in common with the instructors than my classmates), had an exit interview, then went back to my room to pack my clothes and gear. I laid out my Park Service uniform, made sure the brim of my Smoky Bear hat was flat, and touched up the spit polish on my shoes in preparation for the graduation ceremony, bringing back memories of Army basic training.

I returned to the cafeteria for a last cup of coffee before the mid-morning graduation ceremony. I found a fellow Minnesotan, Joe Brickman, a former Ramsey County deputy sheriff, sitting alone and I joined him. He'd taken a job with the U.S. Marshal's St. Paul office, and we'd spent several evenings talking about the old haunts from my days with the St. Paul Police Department. We shared stories of drinking in Alary's Bar, a cop hangout famous for the police cruiser doors hanging from the ceiling and the shoulder patches from hundreds of law enforcement agencies pinned on the walls.

"Hi, Joe. Are you flying back to Minneapolis after graduation?"

"I'm going to Washington first. There's some million-person march protesting something and all the new marshals are being diverted there for a week or so. What's your routing to Texas?"

"The Park Service hasn't given me an itinerary yet. I was told to check in with American Airlines."

"Fletcher, you've got a call," Reg Patterson, the lead instructor, called from the door.

"Maybe it's the Park Service with your flight information." Joe shook my hand. "Good luck."

I followed Reg down a short corridor to his office where he handed me the phone and then stepped away.

"This is Fletcher."

"Doug, I suppose you're polishing your belt and holster for graduation." I recognized Jill Rickowski's voice. She'd been my boss at the Flagstaff, Arizona Park Service office and had hired me as an investigator. She'd arranged for me to attend Federal law enforcement training upon the successful completion of a murder investigation that expanded into drug smuggling and looting of antiquities from the Navajo Nation. We'd become friends during the investigation and had spoken several evenings while I'd been in Georgia. She'd been trying to persuade me to return to Flagstaff rather than moving to a new Park Service posting at North Padre Island. I thought it odd she'd call to make one last plea on graduation day.

"I'm all squared away for graduation and having coffee with one of the new marshals."

"Have you seen today's news?"

"I haven't seen a television or a newspaper since last weekend. What's up?"

"I have a problem. Some hikers got caught in a steep canyon during a flash flood. One ranger and four hikers climbed out. Three other hikers died in the flood. The rescue team recovered four sets of remains."

"They had an unregistered hiker along?"

"No, the ranger is emphatic about the headcount. The group was one family."

I thought back to my last case before going to FLETC. "I suppose the drug runners dumped another of their mules after they recovered their drugs."

"It's more complicated than that. The medical examiner said body number four is a Native American Jane Doe. It appears the body may have been buried, then was dislodged when the flood water eroded the soil away from her burial site."

"Was she an embalmed body that washed out of a cemetery?"

"No. She wasn't embalmed and she died of unknown causes. We're speculating she was buried in a shallow grave. The M.E. said she'd been dead a while."

I thought about the articles I'd been reading about runaways and the number who are never seen again. "Are we talking days, months, years, or decades?"

"He thought she'd been dead more than a couple days, but not weeks. Her hand-beaded buckskin outfit would've been a common ceremonial dress now or a hundred years ago. Have I piqued your interest?"

"It sounds interesting. You and the FBI should have a good time investigating that mystery."

"I was . . . I hope you'll volunteer to come back, at least as a temporary assignment, to lead this investigation. I don't have the resources to handle something like this and the FBI said it's likely an archaeological problem—not something they want to pursue."

"I suppose thcy're still unhappy about my digging in their backyard during the last investigation. I'd like to help you out, but I've already committed to North Padre Island, and I've rented a townhouse in Port Aransas. The moving company will be at my Flagstaff townhouse next week and I've been talking to a couple realtors about listing it."

Jill drew a breath audible over the phone. "Will you reconsider? Please."

I flashed back to the day Jill hired me as an investigator. I was a retired cop working as a part-time seasonal ranger at Walnut Canyon. There'd been a murder, and after vetting me with the St. Paul P.D., she offered me the investigator job. Jill was the best boss I'd ever had, being willing to step back and let me investigate while smoothing over the waves I'd caused. We talked every evening and she liked hearing about the daily progress of the investigation, the details of what I'd done, and my plans for the next day. Through the course of the investigation we'd gone from boss and employee, to colleagues, to friends. We'd had dinner the night before my departure for training and I'd sensed electricity between us, but I'd been out of the dating scene so long I wasn't sure I'd read the signs correctly. I was more concerned about the morality of making a pass at my boss than missing the signals that an attractive woman might've been open to an invitation to have a drink at my house after dinner. She'd called weekly during my training. Our comfortable conversations convinced me that her motivation was staying in touch with a friend, not cultivating a romance. Once I understood the nature of our friendship, I started calling her too. It became clear that we were both damaged goods with a lot in common and we'd become comfortable laughing about the skeletons in our closets.

I recognized the pleading I'd never heard in her voice and my resolve started to slip.

"Do I have a choice, or is this already a done deal?"

"I spoke with the regional superintendent yesterday. He agreed to delay your move to Texas until this investigation is concluded, *if* you are willing. If you refuse, he's going to pull Mark Cochran down from Zion National Park."

"I don't know Mark. Is he a competent investigator?"

"He's young and enthusiastic, but he lacks your experience."

"I'm getting into this Texas thing. Like I said, I've already rented a Port Aransas townhouse and I'm looking forward to exploring Corpus Christi. Hell, I've even bought cowboy boots!"

"I won't order you to come back to Flagstaff, but you're the best resource available to me. I'd really like you to take over this investigation."

When I didn't immediately respond she asked me to hang on. I heard her office door close. "Doug, I need someone I trust. Someone who's seasoned, mature, and willing to grab the investigation and run. I miss your late-night update calls and I miss your cynical, irreverent approach to the FBI. You're more than an investigator here, you're . . . a cog missing from the wheel." She paused. "And I miss you."

I was really looking forward to Texas, but my list of friends was short and I missed her too.

25

"Will you promise to protect me from Sheila, my neighbor? I'm sure she's still looking for a daddy for her boys."

Jill laughed. "If that's what it takes, sure. Whenever she's around I'll hang on your every word like a schoolgirl."

"That'd be a little creepy. If you could stop over every few days and leave her with the impression there is something between us, I think she'd back off."

"Consider it done. I'll call the regional superintendent today and have you transferred back to Flagstaff. He said something about being able to get transport for your return trip. I'm not sure what he meant, but I assume someone will show up with an airline ticket for you." Then she added, "Jamie Ballard, the Navajo Nation officer, calls weekly asking how you're doing. He'll be delighted you're coming back."

Jamie and I had been unlikely partners, thrown together by a Walnut Canyon murder investigation that spilled onto the Navajo reservation. We uncovered a complicated crime syndicate using illegal aliens to smuggle drugs, excavating illegal antiquities from tribal and Federal land, and burying dead drug mules in the excavations. Jamie had been very quiet at first, loosening up as we got to know and respect each other. More than that, we'd bonded over our mutual distrust of the FBI and our distaste for being in the spotlight. We'll never be best friends, but we respected and trusted each other, and that made for a comfortable partnership. It was the kind of partnership between people who knew the other person would protect his back and who wouldn't run away if a situation degenerated into a gunfight.

"Yeah, it'll be nice to see Jamie again."

"I'm glad you feel that way. The fourth body may be a young woman who disappeared from the Navajo reservation. I'll let Jamie fill you in on the details."

"Just to be clear. This is a temporary assignment, right?"

"Let's see how things go."

"I'm already set for the move to Texas." I realized I was talking to a dial tone.

Chapter 5

Most of the students in the class were new Border Patrol or Immigration and Customs Enforcement (ICE) agents. I'd spoken with dozens of them over meals. Most were going to the Mexican border and quite a few were assigned to Arizona. When they heard it was my home, they all wanted to know about life there. Since my assignment had been in Flagstaff, far from the border, I couldn't offer them a lot of insight into the Arizona life they'd soon be experiencing aside from telling them the horror story of finding dozens of migrants buried on the Navajo reservation during my previous investigation. One thirty-something woman was moving from an administrative job with immigration and naturalization in New Mexico after a messy divorce. Like me, she was older than most of our classmates and we'd eaten several meals together. She'd seen the FBI news conference wrapping up my last case. She was excited and motivated about a career working outside the walls of an office and wanted to know what to expect when she got into the field. I gave her a sanitized version of the Arizona investigation and arrests, trying to keep my cynicism to myself. She was assigned to El Paso and when she heard I'd been assigned to Texas, she made me promise to look her up if I ever got to southwest Texas.

There were only three Park Service rangers in the graduation ceremony, and we were grouped together in the last row of graduates. We walked to the podium in our Smoky Bear hats, were handed our certificates (suitable for framing), shook hands with the head of the school, and the show was over. Everyone went to their rooms and changed into civilian clothes. The school had buses waiting outside the dormitories to deliver us to the Atlanta airport.

I watched a young man in an Air Force uniform working his way through the people in line for buses. Carrying an envelope in one hand and a cellphone in the other, he searched the faces as he passed. His face lit up when he saw me.

He compared my face to a picture displayed on his phone. "Are you Doug Fletcher, sir?" He turned the phone so I could see the bad picture pulled from my Park Service file.

I stepped out of line with my suitcase and gun case. "Guilty." I tried not to show my irritation over getting pulled out of line just as I was about to board the bus.

"I'm Sergeant Watson." He handed me an envelope and asked me to follow him. I grabbed my suitcase and we stepped out of the flow of people. "Your itinerary is in the envelope."

I slid my finger under the unsealed flap and pulled out the two printed pages. It started with a Park Service header, then came a simple typed sheet listing a departure time and a handwritten note saying I'd be met at the Flagstaff airport. I flipped the pages over, looking for an official signature and the flight information.

"What airline am I flying?"

"You're booked on a military flight, sir. I'm driving you to Dobbins Air Base."

I grimaced, recalling my flight home from Iraq in a C-130. The center of the plane had been loaded with cargo. The passengers sat in unpadded canvas seats along the outer walls. It ranked among the most uncomfortable experiences of my life.

"This really isn't necessary? I can fly commercial."

Watson picked up my suitcase and the small locked case holding my newly issued pistol. "I'm parked behind the buses."

I followed him to a gray car with antennae on the roof. He stowed my gear in the trunk and opened the back door for me.

"Is it okay if I sit up front with you?"

"Sure." He closed the rear door and opened the front passenger door.

"Why am I flying in an Air Force plane rather than going commercial?"

"I can't answer that, sir. I was ordered to pick you up from the Federal training center and deliver you to the duty officer at the airfield."

"I suppose there's a C-130 crew needing some flight time and the government decided it was cheaper to throw me on an Air Force plane that's already flying rather than paying for a commercial ticket."

"That seems likely, sir. But I really don't know anything beyond my orders to pick you up."

We missed the worst of the morning rush hour, but even mid-morning Atlanta traffic was no picnic. It took almost half an hour to make the twenty-mile drive to Dobbins Field. My Park Service credentials were checked at the gate and we drove past rows of C-130s lining the taxiway. He parked in front of a single-story building near the control tower. I opened the car door and stepped out before the sergeant could open it for me. I watched him unload my bags, then followed him. Inside the door he set my bags down and snapped to attention. A female lieutenant sat behind a scarred gray desk decades older than her.

The sergeant saluted. "Here's Mr. Fletcher, ma'am."

The lieutenant made a vague gesture toward her forehead that might've been a salute. "Thanks, sergeant. You're dismissed."

I felt like I should salute but being out of uniform, I offered my hand instead. "Doug Fletcher. Are you the officer of the day?"

She shook my hand. "Far from it. He's tied up, but he asked me to make sure you got on your flight." She took her cap off a hat tree in the corner and tried to pick up my suitcase. I grabbed the handle.

"I've got it."

"You sure, sir?"

"You don't need to call me sir. I'm a civilian."

"According to the paperwork we received, you're a GS-14. That's an assimilated rank of lieutenant colonel, sir."

I chuckled. "I mustered out of the military police as a sergeant first class. My company captain would be mortified if he found out I was being treated like a light colonel."

We walked to a small plane reminding me of a Lear jet with Air Force markings. A generator cart hummed next to the plane, probably keeping the air conditioning running. "The crew is ready for you, sir." She knocked on the door and it swung down, exposing a set of stairs. A young airman scrambled down the stairs and took my cases.

"Have a safe flight, sir." The lieutenant turned and walked back toward her office.

I followed my bags up the steps and heard the jet engine on the opposite side of the plane start to whine as the airman pulled the stairs up behind us. The ceiling was barely high enough for me to stand up straight, so I bent my head down and followed the airman down the aisle. He gestured toward a seat facing a table. Sitting opposite me was a middle-aged man. His tie was loose, and the top button of his light blue shirt undone. The double-breasted Navy coat hung behind him had more gold braid than I'd ever seen on uniform cuffs. There was a medical caduceus embroidered above the gold braid.

"I'm sorry, admiral. I think there's been some mistake."

"You're Fletcher, right?"

"Yes, sir."

"Please, sit. I'm Peter Holmes."

We shook hands and I looked around and saw two more Naval officers, a lieutenant commander and a captain, sitting in two rear seats. The other six seats were empty.

"Are there more passengers?"

"Only my staff and me." A female airman came to the table and handed him a lowball glass containing two ice cubes floating in brown liquid. I caught the smoky aroma of scotch and it made my mouth water.

"Would you care for something before we take off, sir?" the airman asked.

The scotch smelled wonderful, but I knew having one usually led to many more and I'd avoided hard liquor since moving to Arizona, a decision I hadn't regretted. "Water would be great."

"Sparkling or still? With or without ice, sir?"

"Just a plain bottle of water would be great." When the airman left I turned to the admiral. "I'm a little confused about how I rate this treatment, sir." I buckled my seatbelt and I felt the plane start to roll.

Holmes smiled. "You don't need to address me as sir. Peter is just fine. As for the luxury treatment, we're all going to Flagstaff and we're benefiting from the coincidence of our common destination. I usually fly commercial, but connections from here to Flagstaff are complicated and long. A friend told me you were urgently needed in Flag and our joint travel plans might rate Air Force transport. My aide made the plea and it was approved."

"I've been on Air Force transport in the past, and it involved sitting in an unpadded canvas seat in the back of a C-130. This is quite a step up. I'm not sure how I rate the luxury treatment."

"Silverman said you might have some interesting stories."

I was stunned. "Silverman, the Secretary of the Interior?"

"I heard you were a pretty good detective." The admiral smiled, evading my question.

My bottle of water was delivered as we taxied. "We'll have dinner after takeoff. Would you prefer beef or chicken, sir?"

"Um, beef would be great."

"Red wine?"

"Sure."

The pilot announced that we were on the runway and asked the airmen to take their seats.

Holmes had a sly smile. "You look confused, Doug."

"You're a doctor."

"Of sorts. I don't practice anymore."

"You must be the head Navy doctor."

Holmes laughed as the plane lifted off. "You don't recognize my name."

I shook my head.

"I'm the Surgeon General."

I almost choked on my water. "Of the United States?"

Holmes just smiled.

"You just happen to be flying to Flagstaff?"

"As an Arizonan, I'm sure you're aware of the migrant problems. I'm attending an ICE meeting on the health needs of migrants and asylum seekers at the border. I was told you could provide some background on that."

"I'm afraid you have been misled. I was a St. Paul cop, then a seasonal park ranger. After a murder at Walnut Canyon I was drafted as a Park Service investigator, working out of the Flagstaff office serving Walnut Canyon, Wupatki, and Sunset Crater National Monuments. I have little experience with the migrant issues, ICE, or the Border Patrol."

Holmes shook his head. "I was warned you were humble and didn't think much of the FBI."

The female airman brought out two wine glasses and held out a bottle for Holmes' approval. He nodded, she uncorked it, and poured him a taste. "Very nice." She poured for both of us, then went to the officers in the rear of the plane.

"Do you like Cabernet?"

I took a sip and tipped my glass toward him. "It's nice."

"The Air Force has nice wines. Not great wines, but nice wines." He set the glass down and leaned close to me. "Quit being coy and tell me about your experience with the migrants during your last investigation."

"It was actually pitiful. A drug cartel fed migrants drug-filled condoms, then brought them across the border. They were tired, malnourished, and dehydrated. Once they were safely across the border, the smugglers fed them laxatives to expedite recovery of the drugs. If a condom broke or if the laxatives weren't working fast enough, the smugglers cut them open to recover the condoms. The dead were dumped into antiquities sites being excavated illegally by a couple of criminals."

"You found and arrested the culprits."

"The grave robbers and one of the smugglers died during a chase. The Department of Justice has an informant who knows the details of all the illegal operations. I assume it'll just be a matter of time until the other players are located and arrested by the FBI."

"Tell me more about the migrants."

I waited while the airman set plates in front of us. It smelled like no airplane food I'd ever eaten. There were beef tenderloin tips in gravy, fingerling potatoes sprinkled with herbs, and steamed broccoli, all served on china plates.

"You can eat first if you'd prefer or we can talk through dinner."

I picked up my fork and speared a potato. It was a little too hot, but the olive oil and herb coating smelled heavenly. "I can talk and eat, but the information might spoil your appetite."

Holmes cut up his beef. "My specialty is infectious diseases. I worked at the Center for Disease Control for twenty-eight years, dealing with everything from dysentery to Ebola. I doubt you'll say anything to upset my appetite."

"I'm really not an expert. I can tell you what I saw, but you'll need to fill in the blanks with the Border Patrol and ICE."

Holmes shook his head and waved his fork at me. "You don't understand my position. I walk into the Border Patrol or ICE office and I'm met by the most senior administrator in the facility. His or her role is to put themselves in the best possible light and get me out as quickly as possible. I'll get statistics and generalities, but I want to know the nitty gritty. I'll never hear that from those people, and if I approach their subordinates, I run the risk of ruining careers by cajoling them into telling me what's really happening." Holmes put a potato in his mouth and chewed. "You are my perfect source. You don't have an ax to grind, and you don't have an agenda. What you saw is technically outside your jurisdiction, so none of your bosses care if you give me blunt answers to hard questions."

"If I burn the Border Patrol or the local agencies, I'm setting myself up as a target and if they don't 'accidentally' kill me, they'll certainly not be willing to play nice if we cross paths again."

"How will they know you blasphemed anyone? It's just you and I talking. There's no recording device, and I'm not going to reveal you as my source."

I ate in silence, weighing his words. When I finished my meal, I put my utensils and napkin on the plate and an airman whisked it away. I declined her offer to top off my wine.

"Here's the truth as I see it. There are tens of thousands of migrants coming across the border every month and no stereotype fits them all. That said, most paid a coyote, a guide, to get them to and across the border. They've been assured there are safe places to cross and they'll be taken far inland where the Border Patrol won't touch them. Most everything they're told are lies. The coyotes get them to the border, shove them over or under a fence, and abandon them."

"They take their money and run."

"It's not that simple. Most of the migrants haven't eaten in days. They're dehydrated. Some of the women have been raped by the coyotes and/or the criminals in their groups. They all end up in the Arizona, Texas, California, or New Mexico desert without food, water, maps, blankets, anything but maybe a backpack with a few clothing items."

Holmes nodded while he considered what I'd said. "Then the border patrol rounds them up and evaluates their medical needs."

"Not always. The Border Patrol catches a lot of them, but many, more than half, make it past the border. Some make it hundreds of miles inland and connect with relatives, friends, or church groups. Some of the adults find employers who are willing to look the other way about their documentation or provide them with false documents. The families are sometimes able to stay together; that's a scenario more common if they've already got family or contacts in the U.S.

"Then, there are the girls. They're prime targets for human trafficking. They're often segregated from their families and transported to big cities where they're sold to pimps. By the time they get to the city, a percentage are pregnant, addicted to meth, or have a sexually transmitted infection."

"Tell me about the ones who are caught by the Border Patrol."

"They're dehydrated and hungry. Most of them have some variety of intestinal parasites and a lot of the women want a morning after pill to terminate the pregnancy after being raped on the trip. Many of the older girls, young women, and the teenaged boys, have been sexually preyed upon. They're traumatized. They're physically injured. They need medical and psychiatric care."

Holmes leaned back and considered the enormity of the issue. "I only hear about the hunger and dehydration. You're telling me it's the tip of the iceberg."

"You also need to consider that many, if not most, aren't Mexican anymore. Every one of them is afraid we'll put them on a bus and dump them off at the Mexican border without money, where they know no one, and where they'll become prey for local gangs or drug cartels. In many cases, busing them to a Mexican border town is a death sentence for all but the cunning or the strong."

Holmes loosened his tie farther. "I don't know what to do with this information. If I throw all this on the table I'll sound like a bleeding heart liberal who's trying to let everyone cross the border safely, providing them with medical care and housing that's better than millions of Americans receive."

"You wanted the truth."

"This is a humanitarian nightmare."

"We haven't even talked about the migrants who get hooked up with the cartels and are forced to smuggle drugs across the border. I think they actually have a better chance of making it past the Border Patrol checkpoints and into American communities because the coyotes have a vested interest in getting them past the first ring of Border Patrol security."

"But they're dying from broken condoms."

"That's true, but there are hundreds of migrants without cartel connections who die in the Arizona desert every year because they're sick, can't find water, or get lost."

"And you think the odds of surviving the entry are better for the drug mules?"

"I actually do. The cartels have a vested interest in getting their drug mules inland, where they can recover the drugs."

"The drug mules are dying when their condoms rupture. That certainly ups their risk and reduces their chance of survival." Holmes stopped talking when the airman set two steaming mugs of coffee in front of us.

"Cream or sugar, sir?"

Both of us declined her offer.

The Surgeon General sipped his coffee, then looked out the window deep in thought. His eyes met mine, then he leaned into the aisle and motioned to one of the other passengers. "Lowell, bring your laptop."

The man wearing captain's silver eagles shifted his coffee aside and took a laptop case down from the overhead bin. He took the single seat across the aisle from us and slipped the laptop out of the leather case.

"Lowell, this is Doug Fletcher, from the Park Service." The captain offered his hand. "Doug, Captain Phillips is my adjutant."

As Phillips powered up the laptop, Holmes explained his plan. "Doug has given me some unique insight into health issues of the migrants. I'd like to capture some bullet points for our discussions with the Border Patrol and ICE. I don't want these attributed to Doug, and I don't think we should lead a discussion from them, but Doug has pointed out some migrant issues I haven't heard from our colleagues dealing with the border. I've never been smart enough to ask the kind of questions Doug has raised but now we can drag out some dirty laundry that hasn't been aired with us before."

Phillips listened with his fingers poised over the laptop keyboard. The tiniest hint of a smile curled one corner of his mouth. "Will this information ruin their dog and pony show?"

"I hope we'll be able to force them into a more substantive conversation rather than quietly listening to them throw out statistics about the number of migrants they've processed and returned."

Phillips' fingers flew over the keys, apparently entering a password and opening a file. "I'm ready when you are, sir."

"Start an outline. Here are some softball topics we can throw out: Break down by age and sex. Injury types and rates. Health screenings." Holmes paused while the captain typed.

"Those seem innocuous."

"Then we'll get to the tougher questions. Number of migrants with contagious diseases. Under that heading start a list: Influenza. Norovirus. Measles. Rubella. Mumps. Diptheria. Pertussis." Holmes paused, waiting for the captain to catch up. "Then start some new categories: Human trafficking. STIs. Rape and pregnancy. Parasitic infections. Protection of at-risk youth in detainment. Screening migrants for ingested drug-filled condoms and balloons."

"They're not going to like this, sir."

Holmes snorted. "I don't give a damn what they like. This may initiate the first meaningful discussion we've ever had with those arrogant asses."

I must've smiled or somehow indicated my agreement with his position, because Holmes turned to me. "Doug,

43

what've been your experiences with the Federal agencies? Have they been open and forthright?"

I measured my words, being careful not to make accusations or name agencies. "Many are parochial and political,"

"I like the way you stated that. It's succinct, yet it conveys so much. Doug, have I missed anything?"

"I think you captured my thoughts and expanded on them."

"Lowell, print those out and put them in your coat. When the dog and pony show is winding down, take them out and slip them to me. Make it look like you're trying to be secretive, but make sure they see the transfer. I'll unfold the paper and read through the list. Then, I'll suggest there are a few other topics we'd like to discuss."

Phillips fingers flew around the keyboard, and I heard a printer start up somewhere in the galley. "I can already see them squirming."

"Thanks, Doug. You've more than repaid me for the plane ride."

"There's one other thing. You're also in charge of the Indian Health Service, right?"

Holmes looked inquisitive. "It's within my purview."

"Most of those health issues also apply to the Navajo, Hopi, and Hualapai reservations."

The captain leaned forward. "How so?"

"The population is spread out, many with limited transportation. Most have access to healthcare only when they're gravely ill or badly injured. Lots of people live without adequate sanitation, using hand pumps in shallow wells with poor or contaminated water. Depression is endemic and teen suicide rates are two or three times the national average. Diabetes is a cultural norm and, without easy access to doctors and pharmacies, it often goes untreated."

Holmes nodded. "Untreated diabetes leads to kidney failure, blindness, heart disease, amputation of limbs, and premature death. I know those statistics."

"Those things are all preventable."

Holmes nodded. "All it takes is money and a will to solve the problem. So far, Congress has been unwilling to supply either of those commodities."

"Someone needs to deal with the disappearing Native girls."

"Girls are disappearing?"

"Native girls and young women disappear from the reservation at alarming rates. That's not unique to the Northern Arizona reservations. I watched a documentary about the disappearances on a Montana reservation where I-90 seems to provide an escape route or kidnapping pipeline. Many of the missing are never seen again. Others show up when they're arrested in Las Vegas or some other major city for prostitution or drug use."

"Why are the girls on the reservations any more likely to disappear than girls from any other location?"

"I don't have that answer. I assume it has something to do with the tough life they face on the reservation, and their access to television, showing them the glamour of living off the reservation. The internet gives them contacts and access to people who promise them a shot at the good life, but they connect with people who are just as immoral as the coyotes guiding migrants across the border. I'll bet a month's salary there are at least a half dozen human trafficking rings who prey on displaced runaways they *help* at truck stops and bus stations."

"You believe this issue isn't unique to the Arizona reservation."

"I heard about it in Minnesota, and I watched a documentary about runaways on the Montana Blackfeet reservation. It's not just an Arizona problem, it's widespread."

"Lowell, draft a letter asking for an assessment of the reservation disappearance issue. We can talk about who to copy after the ICE conference."

The airman stepped out of the galley and peeked around the divider. "The pilot says we'll begin our descent into Flagstaff in five minutes."

She handed the paper from the printer to Phillips who carefully folded it into thirds. He closed his laptop, stood and shook my hand. "Nice to meet you, Fletcher. You've opened a can of worms."

"The first step in solving a problem is identifying it. Doug has given us the questions we need to ask. Now we dig for answers and hope we can give Congress a compelling story that'll allow the problems to be addressed." Holmes looked at Phillips' sheepish grin. "I know it's a dream, but we have to try."

Chapter 6

Jill Rickowski waited inside the general aviation terminal as I walked in from the plane. An airman was a step behind, carrying my suitcase and locked gun case.

Jill gave me a chaste hug. "You have a valet?"

The airman set the bags at my side. "Have a nice day, sir."

"Sir?" Jill asked.

"They call all older men, sir."

Jill was distracted by something behind me. I turned and we watched a black SUV pull up as the Surgeon General and his staff exited the airplane. They were wearing their full uniforms and were met by a man in a suit.

"You flew in with an admiral?"

"You arranged it."

Jill shook her head. "No. I got a message from Washington advising me you'd be arriving at the general aviation part of the airport. I was told to provide you with transportation with no other details."

"That's the Surgeon General and his staff."

"The man in the suit who met them is the regional director of Homeland Security. I wonder what they have in common?"

"They're meeting about the health and safety of the migrants crossing the border."

"No one has said much about migrant health issues aside from the children who died in custody of the Border Patrol."

"I think the Surgeon General hopes to delve into the whole issue of migrant health."

Jill picked up my gun case and left the heavy suitcase for me. "You actually spoke to him?"

"He wanted to know about our case with the stolen artifacts and the migrants being used as drug mules. So, we talked on the flight from Atlanta to Flagstaff."

Jill led me to her Park Service pickup and I put the suitcase in the back. I took the gun case into the cab, opened it, and removed the Sig and holster. I inserted the magazine and jacked a shell into the chamber. I put the safety on and slid the Sig into the holster. Jill watched silently.

"It seems strange watching a ranger strap on a pistol."

"You told me Federal law enforcement officers are expected to be armed 24/7. They reinforced that in Atlanta."

"How did you rate the first-class air service?"

"An Air Force lieutenant escorted me to the plane in Atlanta. When I questioned the red-carpet treatment, she said I'm the civilian equivalent of a lieutenant colonel."

"She said you were a GS-14?"

"Yeah. What does that mean?"

"After you left for Atlanta I wrote a job description with expanded responsibilities to rerate you as a GS-11. Someone farther up the chain of command must've enhanced my job description and your position was rated a GS-14. It means you'll get a substantial bump in pay and you'll probably have some training or supervisory responsibility when you get to your final posting."

"I like the sound of more pay, but I'm not sure I want to supervise anyone."

Jill pulled out of the parking lot. "That'll have to get sorted out once you get to Texas."

"Thanks for calling and keeping me up to speed on the antiquities case while I was in training."

"You and Jamie did good work, and I thought you'd like to know how things played out."

"Everyone else in training got calls from their families at home. Your calls made Atlanta a little less lonely."

"Like I said before you left, I appreciated our candid conversations. It was nice to stay connected." Jill paused, like she wanted to say more, but changed the conversation. "You look like you've lost a couple pounds."

"Healthy food and lots of exercise will do that."

She turned onto the ramp for Flagstaff and merged into the I-40 traffic. "I'm glad you're in shape. Our plan is to have you and our backcountry guide hike up the canyon to see if you can determine where Jane Doe's body washed out. I've got a backpack loaded with gear, water, and food for three days. I hope you've got some hiking boots that are broken in."

"I've got good boots, but I haven't slept in a tent since I was a Boy Scout."

"Is that a problem?"

"Not a problem, just a comment. Who's the guide?"

"Liz Carpenter. She was guiding the group who got caught in the flash flood. Because Jane Doe was Native, and because we think her body may have washed down from the reservation, Jamie Ballard is joining you."

"It'll be nice to see Jamie."

"I asked specifically for Jamie because I knew you two had a comfortable partnership. I didn't want to throw three strangers together for several days of strenuous hiking."

"I don't know Liz."

"She's an experienced guide. Most hikers love her, but she makes them toe the line. A few casual hikers have said they wish she'd have lightened up, but the serious hikers appreciate her. She's no-nonsense and serious about protecting the hikers and our park resources."

"Why didn't she know the flood was coming?"

"The rain fell miles away from them and the first they knew was when mud started flowing down the canyon they were hiking. If they'd been anywhere else on the trail they could've walked aside and let it pass, but they got caught in the steepest canyon."

"How's she taking the loss of people she led?"

"She's devastated. We've talked a few times, and now she seems to understand she'd done all she could. The party had a young boy with them, and he was being difficult. Liz had to leave the main group several times to keep him out of trouble. She ran ahead to fetch the boy when she sensed they were in danger. He was a quarter mile ahead of the rest of the group."

"Was he one of the casualties?"

"Liz found him and dragged him up the steepest part of the canyon as the water rose. His mother and grandparents were the victims."

"I'm sure that messed Liz up. She saved the troublemaking kid but lost three others."

"I've been trying to keep her focused on the fact she saved the kid. Without her extraordinary effort, he would've been washed away. Liz was nearly swept away rescuing him."

Jill drove to my townhouse where a Park Service pickup was parked next to my dusty Isuzu. I pulled the suitcase out of her pickup and found my house keys.

She handed me a key ring. "Here are the keys for the Park Service pickup. You know the rules about using your government charge card."

"Yeah. No charging candy bars, soda pop, or chips."

Jill followed me to the door. "Did you cancel the movers?"

"It's going to cost a few hundred dollars to reschedule them for some point in the future, but they're not coming tomorrow."

Jill stood in the doorway with her hands in her pockets. "We'll figure out how to get that reimbursed."

"Come in. I might have soda pop in the refrigerator."

She stepped in and closed the door. "It's too late in the day for caffeine."

"I emptied the refrigerator of perishables before leaving for Atlanta and I don't know if I left any beverages. Aha!" I took out two cans of grapefruit flavored sparkling water left over from my cousin's visit.

I handed her a can and directed her to a chair opposite the couch. "What's the plan for tomorrow?"

"You're meeting Liz and Jamie at the Wupatki visitor center at eight. We'll go over the map so she can show you and Jamie where she dragged the kid out of the canyon, where she found the father and two daughters, and where the rescue team recovered the bodies. After that, you strap on your backpacks and head up the trail."

"Is there cellphone service?"

"It's spotty. I gave Liz a satellite phone, so you'll be able to contact me or call 911 if you have an emergency."

"How tough is the trail?"

"It's rated a moderate climb. It's mostly flat, going across arroyos, over open ground, and through a couple canyons. The climb isn't too bad; it's the forty-pound backpack you'll be carrying that'll be the challenge."

"I lost ten pounds during training, so it'll only feel like thirty extra pounds. In Army basic training we carried forty-five-pound backpacks. In Iraq I wore thirty pounds of body armor and carried forty pounds of water and gear. But that was twenty years ago."

She finished her can of fizzy water, stood up, and walked to the door. "It's been a long day for you. I should let you unpack and settle in."

"My refrigerator is empty. Would you like to grab a meal somewhere?"

Jill smiled, looking like a weight had been lifted from her shoulders. "I'd like that a lot."

I locked the door and we walked to her pickup. I saw Sheila, my neighbor, peeking through her drapes, so I waved. She wiggled her fingers and gave me a half-hearted smile before closing the drapes.

"Was that Sheila, the flirt?"

"Yup. She saw us together on my first day back. That should have her wondering if we've got something going on."

Jill laughed. "Why don't you just tell her you're not interested in a relationship?"

"I don't know. Maybe I'm not as opposed to it as my head thinks I should be."

"Be careful. One weak moment and you might have a couple kids calling you daddy."

"I know. It's been tempting to accept her invitations to come over for a beer at the end of a long hot day."

"Not when you're lonely?"

"That too, I guess. Sheila invited me over for a beer right after I'd moved in. I thought she was being neighborly, but once I understood her kids were in bed, I got a vibe that a couple beers might lead to more than a neighborly discussion of the Flagstaff weather. I flashed back to life with my ex-wife and everything was suddenly back in perspective. I declined a second beer and made a quick exit."

Jill stopped the truck at the end of the parking lot. "What would you like to eat?"

"I ate healthy foods while my cousin was here before I went to Atlanta. The food at FLETC was nutritious but boring. What I'd really like a bacon cheeseburger and fries."

We sat in a booth across from each other and I told Jill about my experiences at Federal police training. She told me about the turnover in seasonal rangers and her struggles to train the new people, molding them into rangers.

"Tell me about the body found after the flash flood. Jane Doe was wearing a beaded buckskin dress. Does that mean she was involved in a native ceremony?"

"Jamie checked with the Navajo and Hopi tribes. There aren't any girls missing from their formal ceremonies. There are some non-native groups who pretend to do sweat lodge ceremonies for tourists, and Jamie speculated she might've been involved with one of them. There've also been reports of a group doing healing and self-discovery ceremonies, but they're not affiliated with any of the tribes.

"I talked to the Yavapai County Sheriff, and they arrested a guy who ran nude sweat lodge ceremonies. He had everyone strip naked around a campfire while he passed around a pipe filled with marijuana, then he'd have them crawl into the sweat lodge. The sheriff had been alerted when a young woman objected to crawling on her hands and knees into the sweat lodge with the self-proclaimed medicine man following inches behind her naked butt. She said it was a scam to get a bunch of naked people high, hoping their inhibitions would be lowered so they'd be open to touching, groping, and more. She bailed out during the ceremony, dragged her girlfriends with her, and called in a complaint."

"I guess that doesn't surprise me. There are always perverts trying to prey on unsuspecting women."

"I've also heard there's a group running a reprogramming camp for people who've been *rescued* from religious sects. The leader's been moving the camp around Utah and Arizona, so he doesn't draw too much attention in one area. The families are paying him big bucks to 'rescue' their kids from these sect compounds and then reprogram them. It sounds almost like a Betty Ford Center twelve-step program to get them to realize they've been victimized and help them return to society. He claims to be some kind of medicine man using Native methods to heal these people. None of the local tribes have ever heard of him and his methods sound half-baked."

"Do you think our Jane Doe was part of one of those operations?"

"I don't know. Those are certainly people who claim to be part of Native culture but aren't quite right. They might put their participants at more at risk than traditional ceremonies. It's something to keep in mind."

"Are seasonal rangers still driving you crazy?"

Jill looked to see if anyone was listening to our conversation. "Despite the lack of privacy in the Park Service trailers, Buck and Lynn managed to consummate their relationship. They were disgusting the other seasonal rangers with their PDAs."

"PDAs?"

"Public Displays of Affection. They were holding hands and giving each other quick kisses when they thought no one was watching. That went on for ten days, and Lynn thought they were in an exclusive relationship. Then Lynn caught him coming out of one of the female trailers. She threw a fit and in response to the commotion, Aggie, the apparent new object of Buck's affection, came out of the trailer tying a robe as she stepped through the door. The name calling preceded the cat fight. The commotion quickly drew a crowd.

"Lynn stormed into my office the next day, demanding I fire Aggie. I tried to calm her down and explained that infidelity wasn't a termination offense. Then she went on a rant about Buck taking advantage of her. She wanted to file a harassment grievance and stormed out of my office. I followed her back to the trailer and found her in tears, throwing her belongings into her rusty Corolla. I watched her drive away, making sure she wasn't going to reignite the fight with Aggie or Buck."

I pushed the remnants of my fries aside and dug my spoon into the malted milk. "Now Buck and Aggie are an item?"

"They never were an item. Buck had gone to Aggie's trailer to ask if she'd swap a shift with him. They'd reviewed the schedule and picked the days they were going to swap, then Buck left."

"Aggie walking out in a bathrobe sounds awfully suspicious."

"We talked. She was stepping into the shower when she heard the commotion. She also assured me she was faithful to her boyfriend back in Ohio. He's finishing up a doctorate, and they plan to get married when he graduates from OSU."

I shook my head as I spooned more creamy chocolate malt into my mouth. "Young love is sometimes hotter than an acetylene torch. When you said you were getting tired of being a mother to these young rangers, this was what you meant?"

"There's so much drama. I end up being mediator, counselor, mother, and sometimes judge and jury."

"I don't think I could handle that."

"It keeps things interesting."

"But you crave other conversations."

Jill's smile faded. "More than sometimes." She slid the plastic bowl from her salad onto the tray and wiped her mouth with a paper napkin.

I nodded. "It's lonely at the top."

"That sounds like an old quote."

"It's from a Chinese proverb. The quote is, 'It's cold at the top of the mountain,' or something like that."

Jill smiled and her dimples returned. "You're full of shit."

"Really! I read that somewhere."

She grabbed the tray of garbage and stood up. "You're not even going to admit you just made that up, are you?"

I hustled after her, throwing the ice cream container into the garbage, barely catching up with her before she got the pickup unlocked. "I didn't make it up."

I fastened my seatbelt when she backed out of the parking spot. As she pulled onto the road she said, "Call me with an update every night while you're on your hike."

"You said the cellphone coverage is spotty."

"Use the sat phone when you can't get cell coverage."

"It may be a couple days before we find anything, and we might never find anything."

"I don't care. Call."

"Is this about enjoying candid conversations?"

Jill shook her head. "The Park Service doesn't like to lose visitors and they're breathing down my neck looking for answers. They know the flash flood was a fluke, but they're using it and the discovery of the extra body as an excuse to squeeze me."

"They're trying to throw you out?"

"It's complicated. Let's just say my position is tenuous for the moment. Sorting out the mystery of the fourth body will ease the pressure."

"We'll be on a fishing expedition. There is no guarantee we'll find answers to the mystery of the extra body."

"All I'm asking is for your best effort. That, and a little babysitting."

"Babysitting?"

"Liz isn't as composed as she'd like me to believe. Her roommates told me she's been locking herself into her room and crying half the night. She won't talk to them and she shrugs it off when I confront her."

"Do you think she's suicidal?"

"I wish I knew. This hike might be therapeutic but keep an eye on her. Make sure you and Jamie know where your weapons are. I wouldn't want her to 'borrow' your Sig and wander off."

"You didn't tell me this part when you lured me back."

"I was afraid I'd scare you off."

"That might've done it."

"Are you sorry you came back?"

"No. It's not like there's anything exciting on Padre Island. It's just a change of scenery. This mystery is intriguing."

"So, you forgive me for not giving you the whole story?"

"I forgive you for now. But we'll talk again after this hike. I may have a different opinion depending on my dealings with Liz."

"Liz is a good ranger."

"You mean, when she's not suicidal."

"I don't *know* she's suicidal."

"You suspect she's suicidal or you wouldn't have warned me."

Jill stopped the pickup in front of my townhouse but left the engine running. "Better prepared than surprised."

"I'll see you tomorrow morning at Wupatki." I climbed out of the truck.

She nodded. "Thanks for the conversation. I needed the diversion from the drama."

"Consider it repayment for talking with me when I was in Atlanta. It was a little lonely and I appreciated hearing a friendly voice. Do you want to come in? I think there are a couple more grapefruit sparklers in the refrigerator."

She hesitated for a fraction of a second. "You need to get some sleep. I'll see you in the morning."

I noticed the flashing light on my answering machine when I stepped into the house. I hadn't checked it earlier and I wondered if there were dozens of old messages waiting for me. I punched play and listened to my insurance agent warn me about upcoming changes in my policy due to the Texas move, three hang ups, a message from my mother apologizing because she'd forgotten I was out of town, and a wrong number.

The last message disturbed me. "Doug, I'm happy to see you're back. Stop over anytime." The caller didn't need to leave her name. I recognized Sheila's voice.

Chapter 7

With my biological clock on Eastern time, I woke up an hour before the alarm. I showered, shaved, and dressed in jeans and a denim shirt. I found my hiking boots and an Army camouflage daypack in the back of the closet. I dusted them off, then packed underwear and socks into the daypack. I assumed my shaving kit would be excess weight that wouldn't be used. I decided a toothbrush and small tube of toothpaste were necessities. After a moment of reflection on my Scout camping experience I flattened a partial roll of toilet paper, put it in a zippered plastic bag, and added it to the bulging daypack. I checked the Sig, ejecting and reinserting the round in the chamber, then slipped it back into the holster. I'd been wearing it daily throughout training and it felt comfortable when I clipped the heavy holster to my belt. I looked at my Park Service badge, trying to decide if I wanted to pin it to my shirt, or leave it in my wallet. Jill closed the trail after the flood, so we weren't likely to run into anyone during our trek. I decided to leave it in my wallet rather than have it tugging on my shirt.

Sheila's townhouse was still dark when I started the Park Service pickup. Continuing the previous night's excursion into junk food, I went through a coffee shop drive-through. I bought a biscuit sandwich and a twelve-ounce cup of coffee to go.

The visitor center was dark and Jamie's Navajo Nation Police SUV was the only vehicle in the parking lot when I arrived. I parked next to him. The cowboy hat pulled over his eyes made him appear to be asleep. I quietly opened the pickup door and walked to the SUV. He pushed the cowboy hat up with one finger. The window buzzed down, and a smile crept across his face.

"Doug, I didn't know if our paths would cross again." He eased himself out of the SUV. He put out his hand and I brushed it aside, embracing him in a hug. It took him a second to put his arms around me, but he pulled me tight and patted my back.

"The captain's been telling people you're like my brother from another mother."

I released our hug. "Why would he say that?"

"Apparently I talked a lot about you after the antiquities investigation. He also said we were equally disgusted with the FBI."

The doors of Jill's pickup slammed. "Do you two need to get a room?" an unfamiliar female voice asked.

The young woman standing alongside Jill wore the Park Service gray shirt and green pants. She had a red bandana tied around her hair and sunglasses dangled from her left breast pocket. She was only a couple inches shorter than me,

64

with a compact build and a deep tan from hours guiding in the backcountry. She moved like an athlete when she stepped forward to shake my hand.

"I'm Doug Fletcher and this is Jamie Ballard."

"You're the dynamic duo who are going to solve the mystery of the extra body." Liz's words were spoken without judgment. She shook Jamie's hand. "And you're the silent partner."

Jamie smiled as he shook Liz's hand but didn't respond verbally.

Jill shook both our hands. "I've got backpacks for all three of you in the pickup. They've got water, dehydrated food, and bed rolls. Liz also has a four-man tent, a stove, a first aid kit, plates, cups, and a cooking pot."

Jamie stepped to the back of his SUV and pulled out a scarred pack, made of heavy canvas with leather straps. "I've got my own pack. But cooked meals will be better than the power bars I packed. I've got room for some food."

Jill dropped the tailgate and pulled out a green nylon backpack on an aluminum frame. She released the plastic clips holding the flap and grabbed a half dozen packages of dehydrated food. She handed them to Jamie, who flipped through them.

"Looks like we'll be eating high on the hog. Stroganoff and noodles, red beans and rice, pasta primavera, and chili.

You Park Service people eat well." He slipped the freeze-dried pouches into his pack.

Jill held out liter plastic bottles to him. "Do you have room for more water?"

"Sure. I suppose we need more than my drinking water if we're going to cook." He pushed things around inside the pack and jammed the bottles in. He cinched the straps tight and buckled them. He checked the straps holding a blanket on the bottom of the pack. "I hope that's it, because I've got a full load."

Jill pulled out two more backpacks. She pushed the smaller one toward me. "There's room for a few personal items in the side pockets."

I nodded toward the larger backpack. "I can take the big pack."

Liz grabbed the large pack off the tailgate and pulled it over her shoulders. "This has my personal gear." The pack was obviously heavy, but she didn't strain under the load.

I hefted the smaller pack with both hands. "Did you load this with gold bars?"

Liz adjusted the straps on her pack. "We each need a gallon of drinking water a day."

"Aren't there some springs along the way where we can refill the bottles?"

Jamie shook his head. "Not that you'd want to drink from. The groundwater is full of nasty tasting minerals and some aren't potable at all. I won't even mention the Giardia in the standing water."

I carried the pack to my pickup and loaded my few clothes, the toilet paper, and toothbrush into the side pockets. I'd been spoiled by my Minnesota camping experience where water was plentiful and all I needed was a filter or some iodine tables to make it safe to drink. I tried to make it look like I wasn't straining to flip the pack onto my back, but the momentum of swinging the pack onto my shoulders staggered me.

Jill steadied me and whispered, "And you thought you could carry the big pack." She handed me one end of a nylon strap. "Buckle this across your hips so your pelvis is carrying half the weight."

I had to adjust the strap length and then fiddled with the holster, trying to get the strap under, rather than over, the Sig pistol. The adjustments made, I looked up. Jamie and Liz had been watching Jill help me with amusement. Both were grinning.

Jamie said, "Rookie," in a stage whisper, winning him a nod from Liz.

Liz cocked her head and looked me over. "He's maybe a six."

Jamie frowned. "A six?"

"He rates as six out of ten as a hiker. His boots are scarred and he's wearing two pairs of socks. Those get him into the experienced and prepared hiker rating of four. I'm giving him two more points for determination and offering to carry the heavy pack."

Jamie considered her assessment and nodded. "How about me?"

Liz looked him over from his scarred and resoled boots, to his backpack and cowboy hat. "Unless I'm mistaken, and we'll know in a couple hours, you're a nine."

Jamie smiled. "Why only a nine?"

"All my ratings are subject to revision based on trail performance."

The weight of the backpack pulled against my hips and shoulders. "Are we ready to go?"

Liz looked at my bare head. "Do you have a cap or some kind of headcover?"

I felt stupid. I unlocked the Park Service truck and pulled on my sweat-stained Minnesota Twins cap, then relocked the pickup.

"Good luck," Jill watched us walk toward the trailhead.

Half an hour later Jamie and Liz were shoulder to shoulder, striding at an easy pace. I lagged behind, looking at the scenery and noting the debris washed down by the flash flood. I took a few quick steps to get closer to Liz. "Where did they recover the bodies?"

She stopped and oriented herself to the landscape. At some point she'd put on her sunglasses. The sun, just above the trees, felt good beating on my shoulders.

"They found the mother and grandmother a quarter mile ahead. The grandfather and the extra body were recovered about a mile farther, in the riverbed."

We hiked another fifteen minutes when Liz stopped next to a tangle of branches lodged against a rock outcropping. "The two women were in that tangle of branches."

Liz pointed to the thickest part of the debris. There were several large branches, probably four inches in diameter at their base, forming the base of the tangle. They were all bleached white, with portions coated with gray mud. I could see broken branches, footprints, and drag marks all around the area. They'd been made when the ground was mud and had hardened into rigid casts in the bed of the dry arroyo.

Jamie shed his pack, then crawled deftly over the tangles. He stopped near the center. "Lots of people were in here. I can see the impressions in the mud where the bodies were caught in the branches."

Liz froze in place. Her expression was hard to read behind the sunglasses, but her skin had taken an ashen pallor.

I walked to her side. "Sit down and take off your pack." My words seemed to break the spell that had frozen her. She took a few steps to a rock and sat down, letting the backpack slide off her shoulders. I set down my own pack and dug inside for a bottle of water. I unscrewed the cap and handed it to her.

"Thanks." She took a few swallows and handed it back.

"Have you been back here since the flood?"

She shook her head. "No."

I knelt down so we were eye to eye. "Are you going to be okay?"

Liz looked over at Jamie picking his way around through the tangled branches. "Does he have to do that?"

"What?"

"Does he have to dig through the branches?"

"Is that a problem?"

Liz took a deep breath. "They died there. It seems like he shouldn't be disturbing that place."

Jamie completed his examination and climbed over the last bit of brush. He sensed something was wrong when he saw me kneeling next to Liz. "What's up?"

"Liz is concerned about you disturbing the spot where the bodies were found."

"There's no evidence to preserve."

Liz shook her head. "It's not that. It just seems wrong to be poking around where someone died." She stood and started walking away. I started to follow her, but she spun around and glared at me. "We've got a problem if you feel like you've got to follow me every time I have to pee."

"No problem," I put my hands up in surrender. "I didn't know what you had in mind."

Liz stalked off toward some bushes.

"She's kinda messed up," Jamie whispered.

"Jill warned me she's been crying all night since the hikers died and she's afraid Liz might hurt herself. She told me to make sure Liz doesn't get access to our weapons."

I adjusted my holster reflexively. I saw Jamie's folding hunting knife in a leather holder on the hip opposite his pistol.

"Three lives are a big load to carry. She must have a good soul if she is concerned that she let them down. We've had a lot of suicides on the Rez over smaller stuff than that. Some of them over stupid stuff."

"The extra body was a Native woman. Do you know who she was?"

Jamie shook his head. "The Medical Examiner is doing some more testing, like DNA comparisons, but that takes time."

"Age?"

"Probably over sixteen. Probably less than twenty-five. The M.E. is leaning more toward late teens because she hadn't developed any musculature or bone density that comes with hard work common on the Rez."

"Did he determine the cause of death?"

"There wasn't anything obvious, like a gunshot wound or crushed bones from blunt force trauma. He's running a tox screen, but that'll take a while."

"Is there anything else significant?"

"She was a couple months pregnant. He's checking DNA of the fetus too, to see if we can identify the father."

"If he's checking the woman's DNA, you must have some families in mind for comparison."

"Several women have disappeared over the past year. We're comparing DNA with their families."

"Several?"

"More than two. Fewer than eight. Several."

"They're doing DNA because you didn't recognize her face at the autopsy."

"I don't do autopsies. The M.E. said her face . . ."

"What?"

Jamie drew a deep breath and blew it out. "Sorry. One of the missing women is a cousin. The body had been attacked by scavengers and then the decomposition and flood did more damage. The M.E. sent me a picture, but it's not one I can show to anyone's family."

"She must've been in a shallow grave," I visualized the buzzards and coyotes we'd seen scavenging the bodies discarded at the archaeological sites in our previous investigation.

"She might not have been in a grave."

Liz walked up behind us unnoticed. "Who wasn't in a grave?"

"The fourth body. Jane Doe."

Liz sat on the ground and crossed her legs with the ease of the very young. "The unidentified Indian woman?"

Jamie nodded. "The medical examiner is trying to match her DNA with the families of missing Navajo women."

"Women? There's more than one woman missing from the reservation?"

Jamie's head bobbed.

"Like, how many?"

"Several." Jamie gave me an irritated look, not happy about having to repeat himself.

Liz glared at Jamie. "Several? You don't even know how many?"

"It's complicated. Some have probably run away. Others, we just don't know about."

I tried to move the conversation to a different topic. "How much farther away was her body found?"

Liz contemplated the question for a moment. "We're still quite a way from the riverbed."

"What's the terrain like on the way there?"

"Above the canyon is more open than here. High desert, they call it."

"How far is that from the reservation?"

Liz shrugged. "The river is the reservation border. She might've washed a long way before she got caught in a tangle."

Jamie sat beside Liz. "Her body suffered a lot more damage than your hikers."

"Damage? What kind of damage?"

Liz's questions came in gushes and her voice sounded increasingly distressed. She wasn't a cop. She led hikers on backcountry trips and our apparently casual discussion of mutilated bodies was more than she was prepared for, especially when three of them were "her" hikers.

I stood. "Let's move on."

Liz stayed seated. "The bodies were, what did you say, mangled?"

She looked at me and I shrugged. "I was in Georgia. I didn't see them."

Liz looked at Jamie.

"I don't do autopsies."

"But you saw the bodies. Were they mangled?"

Jamie put up his hands. "Dead bodies don't look nice. It's not like going to the funeral home where they're embalmed and made up."

Liz braced her hands on her knees and stared at her feet. "I've been visualizing what they went through. It must've been hell. Muddy water swirling around. Branches hitting them and throwing them against rocks. At some point they sucked in a lungful of dirty water and panic set in. Then they blacked out and . . ." She looked at me. "Is that what happened?"

"Liz, what happened before the flood?"

"We were hiking. I heard thunder and just got this feeling something was happening. The kid had run ahead, so I told the adults to go down canyon until they found a place where they could get up higher. Then I ran back and grabbed the kid. The water came rushing through and we climbed a steep wall and got out. When we got to the top . . ."

I tried to reassure her. "What would you have done differently? Would you have abandoned the kid and taken the adults to safety?"

"I don't think so."

"Jill said you almost got sucked into the flood water yourself. Is that true?"

"The kid slipped and knocked me off my handhold. I caught myself."

"How far into the water did you slip?"

"My legs were in the water until I got a toehold in a crack."

"Did you shed your pack?"

"I didn't think about it until I was out of danger and then there was no point."

Jamie shook his head. "Doesn't sound like you were in a position to save anyone else. Climbing a steep slope, water pulling at your legs, with a fifty-pound pack. You're lucky to be alive yourself."

Liz continued to stare at the ground. "I feel like I let them down."

"I saw it in soldiers returning from Iraq. They called it survivor's guilt. Every soldier who loses buddies but survives a battle goes through the same thing. So do survivors of fatal plane crashes, train wrecks, and car accidents. It's human nature."

"When does it go away?"

"It never goes away, but it does get better. The military calls it PTSD and there are thousands of Iraq war veterans who are receiving counseling to help them deal with it. It would probably help if you talked to a professional about what you're feeling. I'm sure there are support groups who could help, too."

Liz looked at Jamie. "What do you think?"

"Talking helps." Liz kept staring at him, waiting for him to say more. Her stare eventually made him uncomfortable. "People on the reservation use healing ceremonies. It brings the community to your grief. It helps to know people are there for you."

"I'm not much into group therapy."

"Some people go on a solitary vigil, wandering into the desert on their own, hoping to find answers and truth."

"Does that work?"

"Sometimes."

"And if it doesn't work?"

Jamie stared directly into Liz's eyes. "Some don't return."

"They wander off and die in the desert?"

Jamie shrugged. "I guess."

I decided to put some hope into the morbid turn of the conversation. "Maybe they find peace and go elsewhere to live out their lives."

Liz listened, then turned back to Jamie, waiting for his response to my thought.

"Sometimes people need a new life to move on."

"A new life?" She asked.

"Make new friends in a different place. Find people who don't know about your past."

Liz nodded. "Hit the reset button on your life."

"Sure."

Liz looked at me, waiting for my response.

"That's pretty much the only thing that works for people with addictions. They need to step away from the people and things familiar and enabling. You might find your answer in the Alcoholics Anonymous slogan, 'One day at a time.'"

Chapter 8

"Did you go to AA?" Liz asked.

I froze as memories of Iraq, alcohol-induced stupidity, my ex-wife, my life as a St. Paul cop, my knee injury, and my dysfunctional extended family all flashed through my thoughts. I didn't want to share them with anyone, especially a young woman I'd just met. I mostly wanted them to stay in the back compartment of my mind where I didn't have to see, feel, hear, or deal with them.

Jamie dashed my hopes of avoiding the topic. "Doug hit the reset button by moving to Arizona,"

"What happened?" Liz asked.

I gave Jamie a disgusted look. He shrugged.

"My life was messed up. I moved to Flagstaff and opened a new page."

"Did the move take care of your demons?"

"Not entirely. At least not at first. I felt a little hollow and lost, but things started to come together, and my emotional holes filled in. I'm reasonably happy now." I paused while she digested my words. "You might not have to go to that extreme, Liz. This walk may be your vigil. You might find the answers you need, and you may come back a different person."

"You think taking a hike with you two might be therapeutic?"

Jamie stood and pulled on his pack. "You're talking. And, you've discovered you're not the only one dealing with some personal baggage. Doug used to be a real wreck before he met me."

"Before I met you?"

"We spent a few days together and Doug talked through his life. When we were done, he'd sorted out his priorities and decided to stay with the Park Service."

Liz strapped on her pack and started walking. I was irritated with Jamie for sharing the things I'd said to him in private. By the time I got my pack on and arranged the nylon strap so my holster wasn't tangled in it, Jamie and Liz were nearly out of sight. I took long strides and caught up with Jamie after a few minutes. Liz, with the heaviest pack, set a challenging pace.

"Thanks for spilling my life story. I didn't realize you were the therapist who got my life turned around."

"You were the one who wanted to talk all the time. I listened like a good psychiatrist and let you solve your own problems by getting them out where you could see and deal with them."

"So, you helped me decide I should stay with the Park Service."

"You made the decision. I let you talk and nodded my head in agreement."

"That's bullshit."

Jamie stopped walking, turned, and looked me in the eye. "You didn't have a clue where your life was going when we started driving around the Rez. By the time you flew down for the FBI news conference, you were a different person. The next day you told Jill you'd decided to go to the Federal training and were ready to move on with your life."

"I sorted some things out, but I wouldn't say you were the catalyst."

"I'm not trying to take credit for you getting your shit together. All I'm saying is that a few days of talking through things was what you needed to move on with your life."

"I would've got there on my own."

"Do you believe that? You'd been moping around your townhouse for months, thinking about getting it on with your needy neighbor. Then we were thrown together and you got yourself sorted out. It wasn't happening *on your own.*"

"Can I interrupt your lovers' spat?" Liz yelled from twenty yards in front of us. "If we don't get moving this hike is going to go on for weeks and we'll be eating cactus fruit to survive."

Jamie broke into a smile and nodded, indicating I should lead the way.

"What makes you think we were having a lovers' spat?" I asked when we caught up with Liz.

"You looked like an old couple arguing about something stupid." Liz took off at a brisk pace.

"I was just clarifying something."

"Was it something important?" Liz focused on the trail as we hiked.

"Not particularly."

"Like I said, an old couple arguing about something stupid. I've seen that enough times to know it when I see it."

I glowered, but she didn't see it. "You seem more upbeat. Did talking about your demons help?"

"We didn't talk about my demons. Jamie talked about your demons. Were you really carrying all that baggage? Is that why you moved to Flagstaff?"

"I moved to Flagstaff because I liked the weather."

Liz looked over her shoulder at me. "That's a cop out. No one likes the Flagstaff weather that well."

"There were a lot of things going on. Let's say Flag is a nice place to get away from the drama."

"Jill told me you'd been a detective somewhere before you moved here."

"I was with the St. Paul police, back in Minnesota."

"You don't look old enough to retire. Why'd you leave?"

"I was injured on the job and they wanted to move me to a desk for the rest of my career. I decided that wasn't what I wanted to do, so I moved on."

"Booze and an ex-wife were part of his decision," Jamie interjected.

I hesitated. I didn't want to share my dirty laundry with Liz, fearing it would become fodder for the Park Service gossip tree. I didn't want to let that genie out of the bottle. I'd been able to keep it capped, aside from spilling some of it to Jamie, and I didn't want to pull the cork again. I was saved from farther discussion when the arroyo ended in a rutted ravine filled with bushes. There was a puddle of dirty water in one of the deep ruts.

Liz stopped. "Here's the Park Service boundary with the reservation. This is the Little Colorado River."

"It's hardly a river." I scanned the dry arroyo.

"It's a raging torrent after a heavy rain."

Jamie appeared, walking up one of the deeply eroded cuts in the dry river bottom.

Jamie pointed to a clump of brushy bushes. "The other bodies were found down there."

"Um, maybe." Liz looked around, trying to orient herself to the location.

I searched for a landmark pointing him to this location. "What made you pick that spot?"

"Look at all the footprints. They sent a recovery team in and they were all over this area."

I studied the ground and saw boot prints in the soil that had been mud a few days before. There were scuff marks and drag marks as we neared the bushes. Liz stood back, silently watching Jamie climb through the bushes. I think she'd spoken her piece at the previous recovery site and knew what Jamie was doing.

"Doesn't it seem odd to you that bodies from two different points would be found in the same spot, Jamie?"

"No." He climbed out of the tangle.

"Why not?"

"There are only a few places with enough debris to catch a body. All the other parts of the river have smaller bushes or are just gravel. The bodies float along until the water gets too shallow to float them or until they get snagged on something."

I looked at Liz, who was ashen and taking deep breaths. Again, our casual "cop talk" was more than she was prepared to hear. Floating dead bodies snagged on brush weren't part of a discussion most people ever heard.

"Are you through here?" she asked.

"Yeah, let's move on."

Jamie turned to the right and started walking back the direction we'd just covered.

I looked around, trying to orient my internal compass. "Why are we walking downstream?"

Jamie paused, looking annoyed. "We're not. The Little Colorado flows north to the Grand Canyon. I'm going upstream. I saw a deeper arroyo coming out of the reservation deep enough to carry a body."

"You think Jane Doe came from the reservation rather than Wupatki?"

"Seems likely. She was Native and I don't know why she'd be on Park Service land unless she'd been one of Liz's hikers."

Liz regained color as we walked, although she'd become very quiet. Jamie was always quiet. Rather than try to initiate conversation, I decided to keep my mouth shut until one of them said something. I gave up after fifteen minutes of silence.

"I've been looking at the debris caught on the hills here. The water must've been four feet deep here."

Liz glanced at the surroundings without breaking stride. "I was farther up the canyon when it crested, but yeah, it looks like it might've been that deep here."

"Looks like it would've taken an experienced white-water rafter wearing a helmet and life jacket to survive the water rushing down here." Jamie surveyed the branches and debris high on the canyon walls.

Liz shook her head. "You're trying to assuage my guilt."

"I'm just stating facts. I've seen people be swept away by water slightly above their knees. This would've been chest deep or more. Anyone without a life jacket caught in the water raging through here was in trouble."

"They were wearing hiking boots and backpacks."

"Unless they climbed above the water level, they didn't have much of a chance. You told them to climb up the side of the canyon, right?"

"The canyon walls were too steep for them to climb where we stopped, especially for the grandparents. I told them to go farther down the canyon, where the walls were sloped and easier to climb."

I assessed my chances of climbing out where we stood as nil. "Were they a long way from the area where the walls flattened out?"

"I guess I'm not sure exactly how far they had to go."

"But, with the water rushing down the canyon, they needed to run to get to an area where the grandparents could've climbed the canyon walls."

"It's hard to say. We were pretty deep into the canyon and the water started washing through about the time I made it to where the kid was sitting. They'd walked a few minutes before the water would've caught up with them."

"Where did you find the father and girls?" I asked.

"It's up ahead," Liz nodded to the pathway ahead where the canyon rose above the arroyo we were walking.

We walked silently, the canyon rising around us as we followed the trail. The flood debris was chest high on the canyon walls, giving me an eerie feeling of vulnerability. I looked up at the blue sky overhead, then toward the horizons. There were no clouds threatening to create another flood. Even that knowledge left me claustrophobic.

Liz stopped so abruptly I nearly ran into her. She scanned the cut into the river bottom to our right and I wondered if she'd seen a rattlesnake or some other threat. I hated snakes. Walking the desert elevated my paranoia.

"I think it was about here," she said. "Yeah. The father and two girls were at the top of little mesa right about here, where the canyon meets the river bottom."

We walked up the canyon a hundred yards. Jamie and I looked at the steep walls. I saw a crease in the wall that looked like it had a few rocky outcroppings I could've used to pull myself out. Other than that spot, I would've been hard pressed to find a way to the top of the canyon wall.

Jamie appraised the walls around us. "How old were the grandparents?"

"I suppose they were maybe sixty. I didn't ask. They were fit and told me about some of the other hikes they'd made. I felt pretty sure they weren't going to be a problem on an overnight hike."

"I don't think my grandma would've been able to climb any of the walls we've passed," Jamie said, shaking his head.

"If they'd made it another fifty yards they probably could've easily walked up the slope to safety."

Liz studied his face for a moment, then realized he'd made a comment, not a judgment. She studied the rock walls and then walked ahead another twenty yards.

"I think the dad and girls must've gone up this chute. There's not really anywhere else to get up the walls here without climbing gear."

I felt the energy draining from Liz and tried to reassure her. "Jill interviewed the survivors. They told her grandma lagged behind, trying to find a place to climb the wall. Grandpa tried to pull her along, but they were making slow progress. Mom went down to help him when the water got up to grandma's waist, and that's the last the survivors saw of them until they heard a shout and saw the three of them struggling in rushing muddy water."

Liz looked stricken. She absently pulled at the bandana covering her head, straightening it and pulling it down farther to cover the tops of her ears. The she adjusted the straps on her backpack.

I tried to keep her focused on our trip rather than dwelling on what happened in the swirling water. "Let's keep going,"

We walked farther into the canyon in silence until Liz stopped again. I looked up the canyon wall and noticed where something had scraped through the rocks and gravel above the line of flood debris.

"Is this where you and the boy climbed out?" I studied the wall and decided if I'd been forced to climb above the flood at this point, I would've been swept away. It's a testament to Liz's climbing ability and the agility of a child that they were able to escape the rising water at this point.

"I . . . I haven't been down here since . . ."

Liz dropped her pack and sat on it, burying her face in her hands. Her chest started to heave, and then she sobbed. Jamie and I set our packs down, feeling embarrassed to be intruding on Liz's personal moment of grief.

When she stood, her face was wet and she wiped her nose on the back of her hand. She stared at the ground for a few moments, then looked up at me.

"I could use a hug, if that's . . ."

I reached out and pulled her to my chest. She started sobbing again. I looked at Jamie who shrugged. He walked away, going farther up the canyon.

Chapter 9

Liz held my hug, crying into my shoulder. I've never been good at dealing with crying women, so I said nothing and patted her back. When the sobbing stopped, she eased away from me, still staring at the ground. She wiped her nose on her hands, then wiped her hands on her green pants.

"Are you okay?" I immediately felt stupid. Of course, she wasn't okay. She'd been crying.

She sniffled and looked up at me, like she'd suddenly found resolve. "I'm fine." Her eyes drifted from my eyes to my shoulder. "I'm sorry. I got snot on your shirt."

I looked down, more out of reflex than concern. "It's denim. It'll wash out."

She looked around with a sudden frown. "Where's Jamie?"

"He was walking ahead last I saw."

Liz opened her pack and pulled out a bottle of water. She took a drink and handed it to me. "We're not doing a very good job of staying hydrated."

"We've been focused on the canyon."

"Dehydration kills whether you're distracted or not. Drink more."

I tipped the bottle back and saw Jamie approaching. He'd apparently been more aware of our hydration because he had an empty water bottle in his hand. Liz followed my eyes.

"I found the spot where your kid carved an M in the sandstone."

"He was a little shit. I should've dragged him to his mother by his ear for defacing the wall." As soon as the words were out of her mouth, Liz remembered his mother was dead and she shivered.

"Mother Earth repairs man's damage," Jamie said softly.

Liz cocked her head. "What?"

"The M will disappear with time."

"It'll take a thousand years of erosion to erase the brat's scratching."

"The canyon's been here a hundred thousand years. It'll be here thousands of years from now." Jamie's head bobbed, as if agreeing with the words. He nodded toward Liz's backpack. "How much farther were you planning to go before we eat?"

"You're hungry?"

"I ate a power bar at four this morning. It's pretty much gone now." When Liz didn't answer him, Jamie shrugged. "I'll eat another one if you guys aren't hungry."

"I could eat something, too," I said.

"There's a spring up the canyon a little farther. We usually eat there." Liz shouldered her backpack and adjusted the straps.

"Is it potable water?" I asked.

Liz shook her head. "No, but there's shade there." She started walking up the canyon.

I lagged behind with Jamie who whispered, "The Park Service doesn't consider any groundwater here drinkable."

"But you don't agree?"

"It's not all bad, but I don't take chances. The springs don't have Giardia or bacteria, but there are mines all over and the ground water is full of the minerals. The EPA is trying to hook up water to a lot of houses on the Rez but it's expensive because they're spread all over. They're handing out filters too, but if a well is contaminated with uranium the filter's not enough."

"How did you find the kid's scratching? All the tracks were washed away by the flood."

"The footprints are gone but there are still signs."

"You found more than his scratching, didn't you?"

"He was collecting petrified wood. There was a little pile where he'd been scratching. The scratching will erode away. Once petrified wood is taken, it's gone forever."

"Take only pictures. Leave only footprints," I recited.

"Is that the Park Service motto?"

"Not really. It's become the mantra of environmentalists and eco-conscious hikers."

"The Park Service should adopt it as their own."

"It's not that simple."

"Ah, yes, the government bureaucracy."

Jamie and I followed Liz. "I had an interesting trip flying back to Flagstaff. I met the Surgeon General."

Jamie didn't respond.

"He's the head medical guy for the country."

"I know."

"I thought you'd be impressed."

"It's interesting."

"We had a long discussion."

"That's nice."

"Aren't you curious about the conversation?"

"It's not any of my business."

"Actually, it is. He wanted to know about the migrants. He asked what we'd learned during the investigation of the drug smugglers."

"Why did he care?"

"He's meeting with ICE and the Border Patrol. They've been feeding him sanitized versions of what's happening. He wanted to know what questions to ask so he'd get straight answers. He thinks he can change things."

Jamie looked at me skeptically. "Can he?"

"He's powerful. He can talk to Congress and get the discussion started."

"Talk is cheap."

I took a deep breath and blew it out. "We talked about health care on the reservation, too."

Jamie shrugged. I recognized the shrug as his response to everything he chose not to talk about.

"The Surgeon General is a good guy. He's not a politician. He's a doctor with expertise in infectious diseases. He'd like to talk to your tribal chief."

"President."

"What?"

"The head of the tribe is called the president. We don't call them chiefs anymore."

"Okay, ask the *president* to call the Surgeon General. He'd like to have a dialogue."

"It's not like the president and I are buddies."

"Leave him a message."

"Doug, you're the one who spoke with the Surgeon General. Why don't you call the president?"

"He doesn't know me."

"He doesn't know me either, Doug."

"But you're, what, one of his constituents?"

"Listen, I have no idea what you and the Surgeon General talked about. Even if the tribal president took my call, I wouldn't know what to tell him."

"Tell him to call the Surgeon General. They need to talk."

Jamie shook his head. "It's not my place. You had the conversation with the man. You should arrange the meeting."

The canyon was open on one side and the landscape turned green. Liz had the one-burner butane stove set up near a small grove of aspen trees. The water was already steaming in the pot when we arrived.

"Stroganoff okay with you guys?" She pulled aluminum plates and metal utensils out of her backpack.

I nodded. "It's good with me."

Jamie shrugged off his backpack and sat on the ground across from Liz without speaking.

"Stroganoff, Jamie?"

"Great. Anything you make is going to be better than a power bar."

Liz tore open an envelope of stroganoff. "You haven't tasted it yet."

"You haven't tasted my power bars."

I set my pack down and sat on the log next to it. "Where do you spend the night when you guide campers?"

"There's a bare plateau ahead. It's sandy instead of rocky and it's elevated so we stay dry if there's rain overnight." As soon as she said the words, Liz looked stricken. "I mean, it's usually high enough. You know, to stay dry if there's a light rain. I've never been there when there's been a flash flood or anything."

Jamie seemed focused on eating. "Water's boiling."

Liz stirred the dried mixture into the pot with a large metal spoon. She reached into her backpack and handed each of us a small metalized straw sealed on both ends. "I call it bug juice flavoring. Pour it into a half-liter bottle of water and shake it."

Liz divided the stroganoff into three portions and scooped them onto aluminum plates. Jamie dug in hungrily. I sized up the pile of noodles and gray bits that were probably rehydrated meat and mushrooms.

I wasn't sure I wanted to eat as much as Liz had scooped up for me. "This is a huge portion."

"The packages are portions for four. Since there are only three of us you get a little extra."

"It may be a little more than I can eat." The stroganoff was actually better than I'd expected, but certainly not up to restaurant quality. The meat had the consistency of rubber and the mushrooms were spongy. I ate noodles and pushed most of the so-called meat aside.

"There are no leftovers on a backcountry trek," Liz pointed at the pile of meaty bits I'd pushed aside with her fork. "They attract critters if we leave them around. What you don't eat has to be packed out and I'm not carrying your leftovers."

Jamie licked his plate while I was only halfway through my meal. "If you're not going to eat everything, pass it over." He held out his plate. I scraped over half of my remaining noodles along with all the meaty bits. He ate it quickly, again licking the plate.

Liz examined my plate when I'd finished eating. "There's a corollary to the 'no leftovers' rule. You're responsible for the residue on your plate. I'll sanitize the plates before I stow them, but I'm not scraping your garbage back into the Stroganoff bag to be packed out."

I nodded my understanding. I used the edge of my fork to scrape up the residual sauce and I ate it. After watching Jamie and Liz both licking their plates, I got the message, although it's harder than I'd guessed to lick a plate without smearing gravy somewhere on your nose or face.

"Where's home?" I asked Liz as she used a tiny sponge and a couple drops of dish soap to clean the plates and forks.

"Arnold, California." She shook off the excess water and set the plates in the sun to dry. "My father retired from the Army and moved to Arnold, in the Sierra Nevada foothills above Stockton. We spent weekends camping, hunting, and fishing, which gave me the skills to become a ranger."

"Growing up in an Army family can be pretty rough."

"Dad retired before I was born, so we didn't move around like my half-brothers. They moved every time Dad got a new posting. He divorced Dot, my stepmom, when he retired. Dot told me they were deeply in love whenever he was deployed, sending love letters every day and calling when he could. They fought like cats and dogs when he came home.

"His retirement was too much togetherness and they divorced. She and the boys stayed in Kentucky. Dad moved to Arnold, where I grew up."

"He must've had a job because half an Army retirement isn't much to live on."

"He got a job in a gun shop. My mom, wife number two, was the owner's daughter and they got married after a couple months. I'm not supposed to know it, but Dot, Dad's first wife, told me I was born early—seven months after the wedding. I never did the math until Dot told me. She did it to be vindictive, but that backfired because I thought it was sweet."

"I suppose the move to working in a gun shop was an easy transition from the Army."

"I guess so. Guns have always been a part of Dad's life. He raised me like another son, and we were plinking at pop cans with a pellet gun before I was seven. By the time I was ten, he had me squirrel hunting. He was tough, and I learned to be safe and to respect my 'weapon.' Dad never called them guns. When we were squirrel hunting, he reinforced safety and accuracy. We had a deal—if you hit your squirrel anywhere but the head, you had to clean all the squirrels. A couple times I had to clean twenty squirrels, and suddenly I'd become a darned good shot."

"Where'd you go to college?" Jamie asked.

"I graduated from UNA."

"What's UNA?" My question garnered dirty looks from both Jamie and Liz.

"I thought you lived in Flagstaff," Liz replied. "The University of Northern Arizona is only a couple miles from anywhere in Flag."

Jamie nodded like that understanding should've been a given.

"I started out as a seasonal ranger while I was in college, working in the visitor centers, and when this permanent job opened up after graduation, I jumped on it. I love being paid to backpack."

"Except for the clientele?"

"Most of them are pretty good. The biggest problem is people who are unprepared for the hiking. They show up with brand new boots and thin socks. Halfway through the first day I'm bandaging blisters and putting moleskin on their feet." She looked at my boots. "Are your feet okay?"

"My feet are fine. If I hadn't spent the last few weeks doing calisthenics at Federal cop school, I think my body would be screaming at me."

Liz looked at Jamie. "How about you? It seems like this is a normal hike for you."

"You're setting a pretty leisurely pace."

"You must've had some hikers who've tried your patience. Dealing with the kid on the last hike was a challenge," I said.

"There've been a few jerks, but not that many. I've rarely had to turn back because somebody was acting up." She became somber. "There was one guy who thought he could share my blanket one night. I woke up with him on top of me and his hand under my shirt."

Jamie shook his head. "That has the potential for an unhappy ending."

"My dad was in special forces and he taught me a few tricks. The guy left one of my arms free when he put his hand under my shirt, so I gouged his eye, then bit his nose while I twisted his ear. When he reared back, I kneed him in the nuts and punched him in the solar plexus. He laid on the ground, clutching his nuts, trying to catch his breath before any of the other campers reacted to the commotion."

"Animals like that tend to travel in packs," Jamie said softly.

"There were five of them that trip. I got the hunting knife out of my backpack before the second one got to me. He made the mistake of thinking he should pull down his zipper before he joined the party. He kind of lost interest when I slashed his face as I rolled out from under him. The others were followers. Without leadership they just melted away."

"What happened the next day?" I asked.

"I packed up my stuff in the dark and started for the trailhead when the sky started to lighten. I grabbed their boots while they were still sleeping and took them with me. I threw them into the bushes as I walked."

Jamie smiled. "Tough walking without boots. I don't suppose you left them food or water."

"I had my usual pack with the cooking supplies, all the food, and most of the water. About sunrise I got to a spot where I got cellphone service, and I called Carl, our law enforcement ranger at the time. He met me about a mile from the trailhead. He took my statement and told me to check in at the visitor center. Jill took me into her office to talk through the details. It was nightfall before Carl brought them in. They were dirty, hungry, and limping. They'd found four boots between the five of them, so their feet were a mess."

"What happened to them? Assaulting a Federal officer is a felony." I had visions of how I'd deal with a situation like that.

"Carl booked them into the Coconino County jail. They got a public defender and posted bail so they could go back to Denver. I told the Federal prosecutor my story and she worked out a plea agreement where they pled guilty to some lesser charge and were put on probation without a trial."

I shook my head. "They should've gone to jail and registered as sex offenders."

"Three of them didn't do anything but watch, and they got off easy. The first guy pled guilty to assault, but there was some justice; he's missing a piece of his nose and he's blind in one eye. I think the prosecutor took that into consideration."

"What about the guy who pulled down his zipper? He should've been charged."

"Have you ever read about the German officers who had facial scars from losing fencing matches? I missed his eye, but he had a cut from the top of his ear to his chin. I think he had plastic surgery in Denver to fix the nasty scar left after the Flagstaff emergency room doctor did a quick stitch job to close the gash. I heard he had some permanent facial nerve damage, too."

"A deep gash?" Jamie asked.

"Right to the teeth and bone."

"Remind me not to piss you off." Jamie smiled.

I listened to Liz's story, stated with bravado. Her cockiness faded quickly, and I saw the slightest quivering in her hands as she packed away the stove and dishes. She put up a good façade but retelling the experience had rattled her to the core.

Chapter 10

"When are you going to start looking for the place where the girl washed down from" I asked Jamie as we lagged behind Liz.

"I've been looking since we passed the place where the first bodies were found."

I looked at him skeptically. "How will you identify it?"

"If the body was buried, it had to be from an area where erosion cut into a dirt bank. If the body was on top of the ground, it's going to be hard to say just where it had been."

"I suppose it could've been in any arroyo or flat area the water washed over."

"Pretty much anywhere and there'll be no trace. The water will have washed away all the evidence. If that's the case, our only hope of finding the place is by the smell. Maybe some decomposition fluids drained onto ground that wasn't eroded."

Liz slowed and we caught up with her. "Jill said you were supposed to call in every day. The top of this mesa is probably the last place you'll get cellphone service."

"Thanks," I dropped my backpack. I climbed the hill, leaving Liz and Jaime in the arroyo. When I looked back, they were leaning close and talking. I wondered about the topic—Jamie didn't engage in idle chatter.

I found one bar of service at the highest point within sight and I called Jill.

"Rickowski."

"Liz says we're at the last point I'll get a cellphone signal, so I'm calling with your daily report."

"Any blisters yet?"

"No, I'm wearing a double layer of socks and my boots are broken in."

"Have you made any breakthroughs?"

"We found the spots where the recovery teams removed the bodies, and the place where Liz and the kid climbed out of the canyon. That's about it."

"Do you know why the dad and girls got out, but the others drowned?"

"The canyon walls are pretty steep. The girls and dad were agile enough to climb up a steep wall, but grandma didn't have a chance. She lagged behind and the water was rising fast. The mom and grandpa tried to help her and got caught themselves. You know, it's really a miracle Liz and the kid were able to get out of the canyon where they did. It's really steep and it would almost take a free-climb expert to make it up that wall. Liz made the climb with her heavy backpack."

"How's Liz holding up?"

"Are you kidding? She and Jamie are practically jogging up the trail. I'm the one who's sucking wind."

"I meant, how is she doing emotionally? I knew she'd surpass your hiking skills."

"We've had a couple rocky moments when we came to the places where the bodies were recovered. Jamie's been good for her. They seem to connect. He doesn't say much, but somehow he has the right thing to say when Liz needs it."

"What's the plan from here?"

"At some point we'll break for the night and camp on some plateau. I really don't know how much farther down the trail that is. I hope it's pretty soon because I'm starting to feel the burn."

Jill laughed. "Wait until tomorrow. Muscles you've forgotten will be screaming at you."

"It'll be just like the day after the first football practice. I can hardly wait."

"You were a football player?"

"I played in high school. I made the varsity squad my senior year, but I wasn't good enough for any college to recruit."

"I suppose the cheerleaders were falling all over themselves to date you."

"The cheerleaders looked right past me. I was too nerdy to attract their attention."

"You were a bookworm?"

"More a shy introvert." I heard a hint of reserve in her voice. "You sound a little off. Is there something going on?"

"Just stupid personnel issues. I'd be so much happier if I could just skip the drama between the young rangers. They have so much energy, but the raging hormones sometimes create situations."

"I'd better get going so we make camp before dark. I'm burning up my cellphone battery." I still had half a charge left. Liz said we'd be out of cellphone coverage, so I could shut it off and conserve the remaining battery.

"Call me tomorrow," Jill said. "The sat phone will get through."

"I might not have anything to report."

"Call anyway."

"Okay, boss."

"Anything new in Flag?" Liz picked up the heavy pack and swung it over her shoulders without waiting for my answer.

"No. Jill just wanted us to check in."

Jamie slung his pack over his shoulders. He held up my pack, so I could slip my arms into the straps. I readjusted the straps and saw the two of them waiting for me.

"Let's go," I said.

* * *

The campsite was clean, as I should've expected given Liz's environmental bent. The flat ground was devoid of plants, and slightly higher than the surrounding desert. There were footprints and a few charred branches scattered after a previous bonfire had been extinguished. Aside from those, the spot didn't look different from any of the other landscape. Jamie was out of his backpack before I'd recognized this spot as a campsite.

Liz set her pack down in the center of the opening.

Jamie anticipated Liz's needs. "I'll pick some kindling."

"What do you need me to do?" I asked.

Liz shrugged. "Nothing." She dug into her backpack.

I looked around and there wasn't anything elevated to serve as a chair or stool. I took off my backpack and sat on it. My bad knee was unhappy about the long hike and being forced to lower me onto the backpack. I watched Liz unpack the cooking setup.

"Chili for supper?" She made it sound like a question, when in fact I knew she'd declared the menu. I had a vision of a bowl of chili covered with cheese, sour cream, and chopped onions. A thick, cold, chocolate malted milk came to mind and would've made my mouth water if I hadn't been slightly dehydrated. I took a bottle of water out of my pack and drank half of it.

"I bet you're daydreaming about a big, juicy, steak covered in mushrooms," Liz smiled, reading my thoughts.

"You're a mind reader."

"Nah. After a day on the trail most hikers are daydreaming about a restaurant meal. I've done independent polling and medium-rare steaks are the most common fantasy."

"An ice cream cone would come near the top of my list," Jamie said as he emerged from some bushes with an armload of dead wood.

"You're good, Jamie. I always send my campers out for firewood when we arrive here and most times it takes an hour for four or five of them to gather that much wood."

Jamie set the wood down and started arranging the smallest pieces into a teepee around a clump of dead grass. He added larger pieces as the teepee grew until he had used about half the wood he'd gathered.

"Are you thinking about using this as a cooking fire or a campfire?" he asked.

Liz appraised his stack of wood. "I think you've got enough for both. Go ahead and light it. I'll set a pot to boil water for supper. We're having chili."

Jamie took out a small plastic tube and unscrewed the cap. He shook out a wooden match, then recapped the tube. He struck the match on a small stone, then cupped the match until the grass caught fire. In a few moments the small kindling caught and he added larger pieces to the fire. I was in awe. As a Scout, I knew starting a fire with one match was the true sign of an experienced outdoorsman. It had been more difficult in Minnesota where the kindling was often damp, but still, it took some skill to start and maintain a fire even in the desert.

I glanced at Liz a couple times while Jamie tended the fire. She assembled a small frame to hold the pot over the open fire. She seemed occupied with her own activities, but she kept an eye on Jamie's fire making. Jamie got up from his knees as the fire grew. He continued to stare at the fire, oblivious to Liz's assessment of his skills.

"Are you going to start supper right away, or do we have time to look around a little?" I got bored watching their preparations.

I got a look from both Liz and Jamie indicating I'd asked a rookie question.

"The fire needs to burn down to embers before I want to cook over it. That'll take a while."

Jamie nodded his agreement. "I already walked around. There's nothing here."

"I've got a tent," Liz patted her pack. "But it doesn't look like it's going to rain and there aren't any bugs. I plan to sleep under the stars."

I looked at Jamie, who shrugged.

"You don't usually sleep in a tent, do you, Jamie?"

"I *have* slept in a tent. I don't carry a tent so I don't *usually* sleep in a tent."

Liz read my face and smiled. "Don't worry, Doug, the coyotes won't bother us and there won't be any other critters around."

"Doug doesn't like snakes." Jamie smiled. "But they usually aren't active after dark this time of year."

"Won't we get soaked with dew?" I quickly realized from their looks that was a Minnesota issue. "Ah. No dew in the desert."

Liz tried to backtrack. "I can pitch the tent if you want it, Doug . . ."

"That's okay. I'll be tough." I smiled. Inside I grimaced. I didn't care if snakes were *usually* inactive at night. I wanted to hear they were *never active* at night. I wasn't getting that assurance. I'd watched a documentary that said rattlesnakes hunted at night, using their infrared sensors to find rodents in the dark. I knew I had a massive infrared footprint and I really didn't want to be mistaken for a giant rodent. Then I remembered seeing a photo of a rattler swallowing a small deer.

"You're not pleased about sleeping on the ground," Liz again read my thoughts.

"I don't suppose there's a motel nearby?" I said with a smile.

"There's not even a porta potty." Jamie grinned.

I almost fired off a witty, profane retort but saw Liz grinning too. I'm sure the words I had in mind wouldn't have shocked her, but I restrained myself. I tried not to use profanity in mixed company, especially while on duty. Our discussion had delivered Liz from her funk, and she was actually engaging in the banter.

"I've heard people use an 'effenheimer' before," Liz said with a smile. "You don't have to watch your language on my account."

I shook my head. "It's okay. I'll be fine sleeping under the stars."

"I had some Michigan campers who peed around their bedding to ward off the coyotes." She and Jamie shared a look and were grinning.

I rolled my eyes. "I'm sure that worked."

"It must've. Not a single coyote bothered them all night."

"Are we going on a snipe hunt after dark, too?" I asked, shaking my head.

"Only if you want to." She assessed the fire, having watched Jamie add some larger branches as it had grown. They'd burned to glowing embers that were better for cooking than flames.

"It's almost suppertime." She set her grate above the coals. When the water started to boil she stirred dried chili mix into the pot. She set the pot over the embers and sat down with her legs crossed. "Do you want me to tell ghost stories or should I wait until after dark?"

I closed my eyes and shook my head. "Is that part of the standard guide service?"

"Only if I have younger campers. Most of the people your age are too tired to sit around the fire listening to ghost stories at the end of a day's hike. You're holding up pretty well for an older guy."

"Thanks." I tried to determine if she was being facetious about my age.

"Jamie, you're welcome to join me as a guide anytime. You're good."

Jamie nodded.

Liz stirred the pot with a large metal spoon until the chili was done. She pulled out the aluminum plates again and spooned equal portions of chili onto the three plates, bringing it to the rolled lip of the plate. Jamie dug into his meal with gusto. I ate slowly, not particularly taken with either the flavor or the texture of the rehydrated food.

Liz watched me picking at the chili. "I don't suppose you have a cold beer in your backpack."

"Sorry, no. I do have a package of dehydrated water. All you have to do is add water to it and it tastes just like it came out of the bottle."

"One smartass remark deserves another." Jamie had already finished his chili and licked the plate clean.

I slowed about halfway through my portion of chili, then held the plate out to him. "It's all yours if you want it."

He happily took my plate, quickly scraping the bottom with the spoon. "If you don't eat, you're not going to have any energy tomorrow."

"Maybe I'll try one of your power bars."

He reached into his backpack and handed me a package the size of a candy bar. I ripped it open and examined the mottled brown bar with deep brown flecks. I tried biting it but resorted to gnawing on it with my back teeth before I broke a piece free. It sucked the moisture out of my mouth like a sponge and the flavor reminded me of beef jerky with chocolate chips. I had to drink water to swallow it. Jamie and Liz watched with amusement.

I looked at the wrapper to see if it was years past its expiration date. I found the date alongside the nutritional information on the aluminized plastic wrapper. It was high calorie and high protein, meant to sustain you, but not necessarily provide a gastronomic experience.

I decided to forgo my earlier decision not to swear. "Tastes like shit. Are the black flecks chocolate chips or mouse droppings?"

Jamie shrugged. "I don't know. I've never read the wrapper. I eat them when I'm hungry, not because I like the flavor."

I threw the bar and wrapper into the fire while still trying to swallow the first bite.

"No!" Liz glared at me as I watched the aluminized plastic wrapper wrinkle and shrink in the flames. "We pack out all our waste." The smell of the burning plastic wrapper assaulted my nose, and I quickly agreed with her admonition to not burn plastic waste.

The sunset colored the wispy clouds pink and orange as Liz cleaned the plates and pot. Jamie added a few more pieces of wood to the fire and a coyote howled in the distance. The chili was rumbling in my stomach and I pulled the flattened roll of toilet paper out of my backpack. "Nature calls."

Liz pointed toward bushes behind her. "Men right and women left."

"Huh?"

"We have a system. Whenever we take a potty break, the men move to the right of the trail and the women go left. It helps avoid embarrassing encounters. Hang on," Liz set aside the drying dishes. She unstrapped a folding shovel from her backpack and handed it to me. "Make the hole at least eight inches deep."

"You're serious?"

"Absolutely. If we didn't bury our waste, there'd be piles of dried turds all over the place." When I failed to reach for the shovel, she raised her eyebrows. "The alternative is a plastic sandwich bag you'll pack out yourself."

I took the shovel, shaking my head. "Eight inches deep. Not four or six inches. A full eight inches deep."

"Yes. Eight inches."

I looked at Jamie, who shrugged.

"Do you have any gestures besides a shrug?"

He cocked his head for a moment, then nodded. Liz grinned. Having Jamie along was cathartic for Liz. I pretended to stomp off unhappily into the desert as they broke into laughter behind me.

Liz handed me a bottle of hand sanitizer when I returned with the shovel. Jamie and Liz were eating candy bars, and they'd left one on my backpack.

I sniffed the sanitizer. "What's in this stuff?"

Liz returned the bottle to her backpack. "It's mostly ethanol. It's about the most effective, environmentally friendly sanitizer I can bring."

"It's like napalm." I rubbed the gel into my hands.

Liz shrugged. "I wouldn't know."

"Where'd the candy bars come from?"

"The candy is courtesy of Jamie. I don't pack anything that's not dehydrated."

I took a bite of the candy. "I thought I was toughing it when we ate MREs in Iraq. They're gourmet meals compared to dehydrated chili."

115

"What's an MRE?" Liz asked.

"Meal Ready to Eat. They're the Army's updated version of K-rations. There's a pretty wide variety of meals and they each come with a catalytic heating device that's activated by water. There's an entrée, a drink packet, and a dessert in each plastic wrapper."

Jamie shook his head. "They're a lot heavier than the dehydrated meals Liz is packing. I'd guess one MRE weighs more than eight servings of Liz's meals."

"True, but we have to pack water to rehydrate the freeze-dried meals." I looked at Liz with sudden recognition. "Every time you prep a meal for us, your backpack gets lighter."

"So."

"So, we're eating something out of my backpack for breakfast."

"If that's what you want to do. Otherwise, I'll make biscuits."

"I suppose all I'm carrying is freeze-dried chili and stroganoff."

"You might have a package of pasta primavera." Liz smiled. "Would you prefer that to fresh-baked biscuits?"

"I wouldn't," Jamie said without hesitation.

"I don't suppose you have butter and honey in there." I nodded toward her backpack.

"Brown sugar for syrup if that's to your taste."

"Coffee?"

"Yup. Freeze dried and highly caffeinated."

I saw Jamie's grin and asked, "This is all funny to you?"

"Liz's dehydrated meals are better than my cooking."

"We'll all be awake as soon as the sun comes up." Liz packed away the dishes and scattered the little bit of water she'd used to clean up on the dying embers. "I suggest we try to sleep."

I looked at the bare ground and the thin woolen blankets tied to my borrowed backpack. "I don't suppose you've got an air mattress in your backpack?" Liz rolled blankets out on the sand.

"There's a foam mat rolled in your blankets." I unrolled the bedding and found the quarter-inch-thick foam mat. It was about two feet wide and five feet long. When I unrolled the mat it immediately curled back up. I watched Liz unroll hers and hold it down with her knees while she spread the Park Service blanket on top of it. I unclipped the pistol from my belt and tucked it near my armpit. I thought of Jill's warning about Liz's mental state and I wanted it close to me, where it'd be hard for someone to take it without waking me. I saw Jamie layer his holster into a folded sweatshirt and put it under his head.

After tossing and turning for a couple hours, I dug the spare socks and toilet paper out of my backpack, wrapped them in a t-shirt, and used them as a pillow. The coyote's howling got nearer and I recalled Liz's comments about the guys who'd peed around their bedding. Then I remembered Liz's assurance that the coyotes wouldn't bother us. After a few more minutes I thought, *they may not physically bother us, but the howling is making me more and more uncomfortable.* I wrapped my hand around the pistol and eventually fell asleep.

Chapter 11

"Look at me."

Positioned with the setting sun shining against the tent wall behind him, the shaman stood in the center of the group. James was the last one to look up, his hands still clasped in his lap, and his ankle loosely fastened to the folding chair by a handcuff.

"James, tell me about last night."

James, a white teen whose family lived outside Denver, looked at the shaman with tired, hollow eyes. "I don't know. We sat in a stuffy hut and . . ."

"Don't tell me what we did, tell me what you thought, what you felt."

James shrugged. "I don't know. I guess I felt hot."

The shaman closed his eyes and pinched the bridge of his nose. "Snowflake, what did you feel? What did your spirit say to you?"

Snowflake, a teenaged Navajo girl, shook her head.

"Go ahead. Say something."

"I felt a little sick to my stomach."

"But your spirit. What did your spirit feel?" the shaman implored. "Did Mother Earth speak to you?"

Snowflake stared at her hands. "I didn't have a vision, if that's what you're asking."

"Did you have visions with your village family before you came here?"

Snowflake looked up with sudden fire in her eyes. "I didn't *come here.* Your thug kidnapped me. And yes, I had visions and I heard voices with my village."

It took the shaman a moment to consider the sudden outburst. Snowflake, the newest person to join the reprogramming project, still showed strong affinity to the religious sect her family joined several years ago. It's been the only life she'd known since childhood.

"Deacon Brian helped you with your visions, didn't he?"

Snowflake shook her head. "I had my own visions."

"Was it your vision that led you to Deacon Brian's bed?"

Snowflake nodded.

"But Deacon Brian helped you with that vision, didn't he?"

"I wanted to be with him. It made me closer to God."

"What did the boys do to get closer to God? How did Deacon Brian help them?"

Snowflake shrugged.

"Now that you're away from Deacon Brian, do you feel closer to God because he took you to his bed?"

Every eye was now on Snowflake. The four others were waiting for her answer. The shaman hoped Snowflake was far enough through the program to understand she'd been raped by the fake deacon.

"I . . . I miss the village. My sisters cared about me. All you do is ask us stupid questions and try to make us feel bad about ourselves. They cared!"

"Deacon Bob had sex with all your *sisters,* didn't he? Think about that, Snowflake. Did that make you all closer to God? Or did that make you victims?"

Snowflake's voice was nearly a whisper. "He cared about me. I was special in God's eyes."

"Why did your parents leave the village?"

"I don't know. They . . . fell from grace."

"How did they fall from grace, Snowflake?"

"My father saw me going with Deacon Bob. He was holding my hand and we were going to the sacrament chamber."

"He stopped you from being raped."

"It wasn't rape! I was being taken closer to God!"

The shaman looked at the boys. "Did someone in your village help you get closer to God by taking you into a chamber with a bed?"

The boys stared at their hands. One shook his head.

"Deacon Bob only helped the village's young girls because he's a pedophile. He only wanted pretty girls for sex and rich boys who could fill his coffers. The others were found unworthy and turned away from the village. You all saw that. You remember the people who were sent away."

The teens stared at their hands. Tears ran down Snowflake's cheeks and she sniffed her nose. "Stop picking on me!"

"Let's commune with Mother Earth. Brother Greg started the sacramental fire. He will purify the air with sweet grass and sage smoke, then we'll pass the pipe. The sweat lodge will help us free our minds from past bonds and allow us to reconnect with Mother Earth. We'll each find our inner selves and learn the way to peace."

Removing a tiny key his pocket, the shaman knelt down, unlocking the cuffs shackling the teens to the chairs. He stopped in front of Snowflake and lifted her chin with his finger.

"You're safe here, Snowflake. Leave the thoughts of the village behind and open your mind to your feelings and Mother Earth."

Snowflake glared at him. "Am I safe like Cora?" She stood and followed the others out of the tent. They began to negotiate the narrow, unlit trail toward the glow of the campfire over the ridge.

A muscular man in a white t-shirt and white canvas pants sidled up to the shaman after the patients passed. "This group is fucked up. They saw us carry the girl out of the igloo and they all know something happened to her."

"Shh. It's a sweat lodge not an igloo, you idiot. They know nothing. I told them we took Cora to the hospital."

"They know the van never left camp. I bet they even heard me digging."

Chapter 12

The sun was shining in my eyes when I awoke, feeling like I'd barely fallen asleep. The foam pad rolled itself up as soon as I sat up. The wool blanket felt good around my shoulders in the crisp morning air while I mentally shook off the last vestiges of sleep.

Liz and Jamie sipped coffee from metal cups next to a fire already burned down to coals. The aroma of coffee and biscuits filled the chilly morning air. I stood, but the movement wasn't graceful. The aching muscles Jill had predicted were fully evident. The hip that had been against the ground ached.

Jamie glanced at me. "The dead have arisen."

Liz took a pot off the fire and carefully poured boiling water into a metal cup. She scooped a teaspoon of instant coffee from a plastic zipper bag and stirred it into the water.

"Be careful with the aluminum until it cools off." She passed the cup to me, holding the brim carefully.

"I learned that lesson when I was a Scout."

"And you still remember it," she said with a smile. "It must've been a painful experience."

"I burned my fingers and lips, then scalded my tongue. That's an experience that stays with you."

Jamie nodded. "Experience is a tough teacher. You don't get the lesson until after the test."

"Confucius?" I asked.

"I don't know where I heard it. I just know it's true."

Liz pulled a Dutch oven out of the coals and lifted the lid. My mouth started to water and my stomach told me I'd only eaten partial rations yesterday. She skillfully lifted golden biscuits with a fork and set three on each plate. She handed me an aluminum cup with dark liquid.

"It's brown sugar syrup."

I split my biscuits and drizzled syrup over them. She uncovered another pan and scooped scrambled eggs onto my plate.

"I suppose it's too much to hope that you actually packed eggs in your backpack."

"You're right." She handed me little plastic salt and pepper containers. "We don't want to take a chance packing unrefrigerated eggs. The last thing you want on a backcountry trip is a case of salmonella."

I ate the rehydrated eggs quickly, then savored the warm biscuits. The biscuit and brown sugar flavor covered the nasty taste the eggs left in my mouth. By the time I wiped my plate clean with the last piece of biscuit, Jamie was eating the crumbs he'd scraped from the biscuit pan.

"I think Jamie likes your cooking, Liz."

Jamie, his mouth full of crumbs, nodded. "I like anyone else's cooking. Liz, you're doing an excellent job with what you've got for ingredients. These biscuits are better than my grandmother made."

Liz smiled, appreciating the compliment. She poured more hot water in each of our cups and passed the instant coffee around.

"Aside from a few petroglyphs just ahead, this is as far as I've ever taken this trail." Liz scraped the egg pan onto Jamie's plate.

I was relieved she hadn't offered me seconds. "How far away is the reservation, Jamie?"

"Hard to say."

"Could you guess?" I was somewhat irritated by his reply.

"Maybe another twenty minutes of hiking. You know, the border is just a line on a map. It's not spray-painted on the ground."

"I thought maybe there'd be a fence."

"No fence. The Little Colorado River is the dividing line."

Liz cleaned all the dishes and set them out to dry. She looked around the landscape, then took a roll of toilet paper out of her backpack and grabbed the shovel.

I patted my backpack. "I have cushioned toilet paper. The commercial with the bears says it cleans better."

"I like the quilted brand." She walked off toward a bush-screened area on the opposite side of the trail from the area I'd chosen the night before.

"What's the plan, Jamie?"

"We walk."

"Yes, we walk. But which direction and what are we looking for?" I spoke a little too testily, regretting my tone as soon as the words were out. Jamie seemed unfazed by my sharp comments.

"I think we'll follow the deepest arroyo. It seems like it'd have the heaviest flow of water—enough to carry a body. Most of the others are too small. Some of the brush washed down them, but not a woman."

I nodded, seeing the wisdom in his analysis. "Sorry I snapped at you."

"You're tired and sore."

"Thank you."

"Thanks for what?" Liz asked, reappearing with the toilet paper and shovel. "Are you handing out more candy bars, Jamie?"

Liz squirted sanitizer on her hands while Jamie dug in his pack. "I've only got a few more." He handed one to each of us. "When the last of these are gone we'll have to eat power bars for dessert."

He gave me a sly look, just to let me know he was yanking my chain. I wasn't eating another power bar unless

I was starving. Liz opened the empty dried egg bag to collect our candy bar wrappers, folded it up, and put it into a side pocket of her backpack.

"Are we ready to roll?" Liz asked.

"Give me a second." I examined my coiled foam pad and the blanket spread on the ground. Jamie and Liz had rolled up their sleeping kits and they were neatly tied to their packs.

I felt clumsy and it took two tries to get the foam pad and blanket rolled tight enough to fit in the short straps on the bottom of my pack. I stowed my sock/pillow back into a side pocket of the pack. Somehow the pack had gained weight from what I remembered. I wondered briefly if Liz and Jamie had slipped water bottles into my pack while I'd slept, then reasoned that the problem was entirely my tired and sore muscles. Jamie and Liz seemed unaffected by the previous day's trek, shouldering their packs with ease.

When I looked up, they were grinning. "What?"

"Are you about ready?" Jamie asked, standing with his pack already on his back.

An hour later we stopped at the petroglyphs, ancient markings carved into the stone, a quarter mile from the campsite. Liz said they were a combination of artistic work and representations of ancient life. Jamie stared at one with his head cocked.

"What do you see?" I moved alongside him.

"Looks kinda pornographic." He studied the images from a couple angles.

Liz joined us. "Yup, the ancient people recorded every aspect of human life at one site or another." She paused. "They weren't introduced to the missionary position until some later time."

"Or, the one on the bottom isn't a woman." Jamie shrugged and stepped away.

Liz rolled her eyes. "Why'd you have to say that? I'll never look at that image the same way again."

"I'm just saying there's another possibility."

I lagged behind, half listening to the two of them talk and half watching the landscape for a burial spot. Jamie would see it first, if we came across one, but I tried to be vigilant.

A half hour later we found a large rockpile next to a shallow hole. It had markings from excavation by a mechanical device. Jamie and Liz circled the pile and looked at the shallow hole maybe fifty by twenty yards. Based on the rings around the perimeter, it had contained water at some time. The bottom was now dry.

"This looks like a mining operation." I took the opportunity to set down my pack and roll my shoulders.

"There are lots of old holes. This area has rich uranium deposits and there was mining on both the Rez and private land during the cold war." Liz recited the story like she'd told it to tour groups a thousand times.

"Are we in danger from the radiation?"

"No." Jamie shook his head. "All the high-grade ore is gone and what's left isn't dangerous unless you're exposed continuously."

"The EPA is working with the Navajo Nation to clean up the worst sites," Liz said. "There are some mine buildings being demolished and the hotspots are being covered."

Jamie slid his pack off and sat on it. "The bigger problem is people raiding the old mines for building materials. Blocks, sheet metal, and plywood are expensive and hard to come by on the Rez. People take pickup loads of stuff away and incorporate it into their homes and livestock corrals. The EPA and tribal leaders are trying to educate people, but they see concrete blocks and they're too tempting to leave alone."

"Then what happens?" I knew the answer.

"The tribal people have high rates of lung cancer, kidney failure, diabetes, and other cancers. Some of that is genetic and lifestyle related, but lots of it is due to the uranium and wells contaminated with heavy metals."

"Do you think that's what killed our woman?" I asked.

Liz set her pack down too, giving up on her hope of moving us along quickly. "Probably not. Those deaths are caused by prolonged exposure and tend to strike people in middle age or later. Our woman was killed by an acute cause."

I was surprised Jamie wasn't answering. Liz was doing a good job answering the questions, probably because of her guide knowledge. Jamie just stood by listening to her explanations without comment.

I looked around. "I take it we're on the reservation now. I assume there aren't any mines on the national monument."

"A lot of the mines that pre-date the national monument," Liz explained. "There have been prospectors here forever. The ancient tribes dug up turquoise and flint. Then the Spaniards came looking for gold and silver."

"The Spaniards didn't do any mining." Jamie corrected her. "They just stole what they wanted and moved on."

Liz nodded. "Then the whites came looking for gold. There wasn't any gold here, so the government created the reservations. The prospectors came back in the '50s looking for uranium. They weren't particular about land ownership, and they posted claims on any piece of land that looked like a promising mine."

"Yeah, and the government was so anxious to get uranium for the arms race they ignored treaties, mineral rights, and Park Service boundaries," Jamie added. "By the way, the Little Colorado River was the gully we crossed a while back. That's the dividing line between the reservation

131

and the Park Service land. There are old mining operations on both sides of the river."

As we walked farther onto the reservation and gained altitude the land became more sculpted. I was looking at juniper trees on the hills when a flash caught my eye. I stared at the spot for a few seconds and saw it again. It was so bright it had to be the sun reflecting off glass or metal. I tried to not act alarmed but sped up and drew even with Jamie.

"Someone's watching us." I tried not to look like we were aware of the surveillance.

"Yup."

"How long has he been watching?

"I saw him about the time we crossed onto the Rez."

"Were you going to mention it to me?"

"Why? No law against looking at people through binoculars."

"What if he had something to do with the woman's death?"

"I'd say it's a fifty-fifty chance. Not many people on this part of the Rez. If he doesn't know what happened to her, he probably knows someone who does."

"Are you planning to ask him?"

"Yup."

"Soon?"

"I figured I walk up there when we stop for lunch. You and Liz can make lunch and I'll pretend to go looking for kindling. I'll slip behind him and see who it is."

"You don't think he'll see you and run?"

"It's doubtful."

Liz was a few steps ahead so I sped up. "Don't stop walking but listen to me."

"What?" she asked, immediately stopping.

I grabbed her arm and propelled her along. "There's someone in the hills watching us. Jamie's going to sneak around behind him while you and I prep lunch."

"Do you want to stop now?" Her eyes scanned the surrounding hills.

"Jamie, is it lunchtime?"

"Sure." He was a man of few words except for his discussions with Liz.

He pointed to an open spot and we dropped our backpacks. Jamie gathered a few sticks and started a fire. Then he left for some bigger branches. Liz broke out the butane stove and attached a red fuel bottle to it. She started heating water.

"Let's use the pasta primavera from your pack, Doug."

"Sounds better than I expect the finished product will taste." I pulled the pouch out and handed it to Liz.

"It's actually one of our better options," Liz said, readying the aluminum plates and utensils. "What flavor of bug juice would you like with lunch?"

"Do you have grape?"

"Your wish is my command." She dug into her backpack and handed me a purple straw sealed on both ends. I tore off one end and poured the powder into a half liter of water. It tasted heavenly.

The fire died down so I wandered in the opposite direction from Jamie's departure and gathered a few medium-sized branches. They caught quickly and the campfire grew. Liz stirred the pasta mix into the boiling water, then I heard a gunshot. She looked at me with concern.

"That sounded like a .22 rifle. You and Jamie may be outgunned."

"Let's hope Jamie's smarter than the person with the rifle." Almost immediately we heard a volley of three shots, obviously from a different gun.

"Jamie?"

"Probably. I don't suppose you've got a couple bullet-proof vests in your backpack," I pushed myself up and instinctively checked to make sure the Sig pistol was still on my hip.

She looked nervously up the hill, toward the sound of the gunshots. "Bulletproof vests haven't been an issue before."

"Pull out the sat phone and call Jill. Give her our position and report there've been shots fired."

Liz pulled the cooking pot off the stove, then dug the sat phone out of her backpack. "Since we're on the reservation, shouldn't we call the Navajo police?" she asked while the phone powered up.

"Call them after you talk to Jill."

I was torn between staying to protect Liz and going up the hill to provide backup for Jamie. Jamie's backup became the priority when we heard another shot from the .22. I trotted uphill, in the direction of the shots. My trot lasted maybe a hundred yards, then it became a quick step. That dropped to a plodding pace as I neared the sound of the shooting. Not knowing exactly where the shots had originated, I stayed low and used the rocks and bushy trees for cover, keeping my eyes trained above me for signs of movement. I stumbled often but managed to stay on my feet. After fifteen minutes I regretted not grabbing a bottle of water before running off.

Another shot rang out, not far from where I was in a gully. I ducked down and waited. After a moment I heard a man cough. He sounded quite a bit farther up the hill. I pulled my Sig and crept up a shallow ravine, trying to keep my head down. Every twenty yards or so, I'd pop up and look for a sign of Jamie or the shooter. The coughing came frequently and kept me apprised of the shooter's position. The ravine got shallower as I went higher, and I got to a point where it didn't provide cover. Sadly, it was also very close to the sound of the coughing. I darted from bush to bush until I was close to the last place I'd heard coughing. I caught my breath behind a thick juniper and rationalized it wouldn't provide protection from a bullet, but a shooter wouldn't know exactly where I was behind the tree, which improved my odds of not being hit. A second thought brought me to the stupidity of my flimsy cover and I started searching for something solid ahead.

The coughing was close now. I stuck my head around the side of the juniper tree and studied the rocky, bushy slope above. The shooter coughed again, and I focused on a clump of bushes about fifty yards up the slope. I saw brown that didn't match the gray/green of the bush. The longer I stared I thought I might just be seeing gravel behind the bushes. The coughing continued, but I couldn't identify the outline of a person. I darted to the next rocky outcropping, hoping I was as invisible as the shooter. In Army basic training they taught us that movement was what usually caught a sniper's eye. I hoped to see him before my climb up the slope or my blue denim shirt and pants revealed my presence to the shooter.

I stopped behind a large bush more than halfway up the slope and saw Jamie, prone behind a boulder about thirty yards ahead of me. His feet were toward me, he wasn't moving, and there was bright crimson blood on the shoulder of his uniform shirt.

I darted ahead and took cover behind a rock the size of a Volkswagen and felt pretty secure. I was tempted to call out to Jamie, but in case I'd somehow managed to approach without being seen, I decided to just peek up the hill to try and spot the gunman again. I heard coughing directly above me, so I peeked around the rock, quickly scanned the hill, then pulled back. I'd seen nothing but rocks and trees. The clump of bushes with the brown patch wasn't far away, but I still couldn't identify a person in them. I decided to take another quick look at the suspicious bushes before sprinting to Jamie. My nose had barely cleared the edge of my hiding spot when a bullet ricocheted off the rock under my chin. I heard the 'crack' of the rifle at the same time the bullet struck before whining away. I'd broken a foot soldier's first rule: When trying to spot the enemy, don't stick your head out twice in the same place.

Jamie shifted so I could see his face. He'd apparently been watching for the gunman. He glared at me and gave me a gesture I took to mean, "What are you doing?"

Again, I heard coughing above us. I wondered if one of Jamie's shots had hit the guy in a lung and he was bleeding out.

Chapter 13

Jamie sat up and braced his back against the boulder. "Navajo Nation Police! Put down your weapon and come out with your hands up!"

We waited for a response, but heard nothing for a few moments, then another cough. The shooter was moving down the hill.

Jamie sprinted across the space between our positions and slid in next to me. The shoulder of his shirt was bloody with a tiny hole that had penetrated his shirt about halfway across top of his left shoulder. He held his left arm tight against his chest.

"What are you doing, Doug?" He asked before I could inquire about his shoulder wound.

"We heard gunfire."

"You left Liz alone and unarmed?"

"I thought I should back you up." Again we heard coughing, this time from even farther down the hill. "Did you hit that guy?"

"I think he's just sick. I was stalking him and had been following his cough as he worked his way above our camp. I'm pretty sure he's been watching us since we crossed onto the Rez. I made the rookie mistake of moving too fast and getting caught with my silhouette sky-lined on a ridge."

The coughing got fainter and farther down the hill. "I told Liz to call the Park Service and your department on the sat phone. Maybe help will be on the way."

"I've got news for you; backup isn't going to be here in time to save us." Jamie sprinted from behind the rock. After a few seconds he stopped behind a juniper and waved me down while he kept his gun trained on the rocky cover below us. We heard another cough, farther away. I followed behind, loping along, stumbling over rocks and twigs, then finally falling on my face when I caught my boot on a root.

"Can you make any more noise?" Jamie hissed, giving me a disgusted look.

I got up and dusted off my shirt. I inspected the Sig for damage, then slid the action to check the round in the chamber. The coughing was much farther down the hill.

"Keep me covered while I make another move," Jamie said.

We continued down the hill, Jamie leapfrogging ahead while I kept my gun trained on the area below us. The trees thinned to bushes and the boulders above became rocks. We finally got to the open arroyo below us. Liz sat on her backpack with her hands in the air. A young man, dressed in a brown Carhartt coat, pointed a rifle at her. His coat was the brown I'd seen behind the bushes. They were only thirty yards away when Jamie and I took cover behind the last clump of bushes on the slope.

"Come out where I can see you," the man yelled. Jamie gave me a resigned look and I felt shitty about having abandoned Liz. I should've put my trust in Jamie's skills and made sure Liz was safe. On the other hand, Jamie had been shot with blood still oozing onto his shirt, although the wound didn't seem to be slowing him down. I wondered if I hadn't shown up whether the two of them might've been in a standoff on the hill until Jamie became lightheaded and passed out.

Jamie stepped out with his right hand in the air, his gun held high, but with his fingers open, showing he wasn't gripping it or preparing to shoot. He moved toward our campsite. I watched from behind the bushes, waiting to see how Jamie's move played out.

The man had a coughing fit and could barely keep the gun pointed at Liz. "Where's the other guy?" he asked, wiping the spit from his mouth on the sleeve of his coat.

"He's still coming down the hill."

"Set your gun down and walk over here."

Jamie bent down and gently set his pistol in the dirt. Then he walked toward Liz and the armed man.

"Put both your hands up." The yelling triggered another coughing fit.

"I can't. You shot me in the shoulder," Jamie said, walking into the campsite. "I think my collarbone is broken. I can't lift my arm."

"Sit there." The man pointed to an open area away from the campfire and our backpacks. "Who's the other guy?"

"He's a Park Service ranger, like our cook." Jamie spoke loud enough for me to hear. "Doug! Come down. He's got a gun on Liz."

I pulled my holster off my belt and put the spare magazine in my left pocket. I lifted the tail of my shirt and tucked the Sig in the small of my back where it would be out of sight, then dropped the shirttail over it. I set the holster and my wallet with my badge and investigator I.D. on the ground behind a rock, then walked into the opening with my hands over my head.

"Come down here and sit next to the Indian cop."

I walked into the campsite and sat down next to Jamie.

Every minute or two the guy had a coughing fit. His skin was gray and he looked gaunt, his clothes hung on him like he'd lost weight.

"Throw me your wallet," he said, eyeing me suspiciously.

"I left it at the Wupatki visitor center in my truck. My keyring is in the green backpack."

"If you're a ranger, why aren't you in uniform like the cook?"

"I'm off duty. This trip was supposed to be a vacation on my days off."

He had another coughing fit while he seemed to be thinking about what I'd said. He squirmed and itched his belly.

He motioned for Liz to stand up with the rifle. "Dump the ranger's backpack."

She got up slowly and turned the backpack upright, then untied the cover flap. She started to lift out the contents, one item at a time.

"Just dump it out!" he yelled, getting impatient. He coughed again and scratched at his neck. I began to think he had some kind of rash irritating his skin.

The contents spilled onto the ground. Dirty socks came out first, then two bottles of water and packages of freeze-dried food. "Give me some water," he ordered Liz, keeping the gun generally pointed at Jamie and me.

Liz carried the water over and stopped when he swung the gun around and pointed it at her. "Just set it down there and roll the bottle to me."

"I cooked a pot of pasta if you're hungry, Liz said as she rolled the water to the guy.

"Yeah. Pile some food on a plate." He squirmed like he was sitting on an ant hill.

Liz pulled out the bottle of hand sanitizer, which caused the man to raise the gun ominously. I saw Jamie tense, maybe preparing to make a lunge at the guy if Liz was in serious jeopardy.

"You'd best clean up your hands before you eat." She held the sanitizer out, but the guy signaled for her to stop.

"Just toss it here."

I could barely believe what I was seeing. Liz was calm, but it seemed surreal that she'd have the guy sanitize his hands.

The guy put the rifle across his lap and squeezed sanitizer onto his grimy hands, then set the bottle at his feet, near the dying fire. Liz scooped a pile of the pasta onto a plate, stuck a fork into it. She pushed it across the ground toward the guy.

"I'll bet the Indian cop has handcuffs. Dump out his backpack."

Liz walked to Jamie's backpack, searching his face for any sign she shouldn't comply. Jamie gave her a just perceptible nod. She unstrapped the leather tabs and upended the backpack. Smaller bottles of water fell out with clothing, packages of dehydrated food, power bars, and several sets of plastic ties that were handcuffs. The last things to fall out were candy bars.

The man's face lit up when he recognized the logo on the wrappers.

"Throw me those candy bars. Then you go over there and handcuff the two guys behind their backs."

She walked to where Jamie and I were sitting. "What should I do?" she whispered as she knelt behind us.

"There's a knife in a case on my left hip. Just slide the case so I'll be able to reach it with my hands in cuffs."

"Quit your whispering," the guy yelled, waving the rifle at us.

"I've never used these things before. It'll take a second," Liz yelled back.

She threaded the plastic cuffs loosely around Jamie's wrists, then bent down behind me. Her knee pushed against Jamie's knife case and it slid back until it hit the loop over his wallet.

I tilted my head down and leaned forward, making it easy for Liz to cuff me. "There's a gun in my waistband. Slip it into your boot."

I felt the gun leave my waistband, then I felt the plastic cuffs on my wrists. She'd left them loose so I could pull my hands free when it was time to make our move. Liz blocked the guy's view of Jamie's hands while she cuffed me, and Jamie opened the knife case and flipped the knife open.

"Your gun's too bulky. It won't fit in my boot," Liz whispered.

"How about your back pocket or the back of your waistband?"

The guy wolfed down the pasta, while balancing the rifle across his knees, coughing and itching. When Liz returned to the campfire, he tossed the plate back to her. After another coughing fit, he told her to refill the plate. Jamie wiggled free of the cuffs and held the knife ready for an attack. Bringing a knife to a gunfight is never a good idea, but sometimes you do the best you can with what you have.

"We've got help coming," I said to the gunman. "You need to see a doctor about that cough."

"I'm not going to no doctor. You'll just arrest me and throw me in jail for running off with Mandy."

"Mandy Dove?" Jamie asked. "She's with you?"

"We were going to hang out in the hills until people stopped looking for her, then we were going to find a minister to marry us."

"Her family has been worried about her," Jamie said.

"Yeah? Well they weren't too pleased she was dating a white guy. They should've known she wasn't going to stop seeing me just because they said so."

"Where's Mandy?" I asked.

"We got this cough and she couldn't get rid of it. We knew the cops would be looking for me 'cause she wasn't eighteen, so we couldn't go to a doctor in town." He had another coughing fit that took his breath away. He took a deep breath and seemed to relax.

Jamie shifted his weight forward, preparing to jump up and rush the gunman. "Sounds like she maybe needs some medicine if she's coughing like you."

"Yeah, well, that wasn't going to happen. She started coughing blood and the next day she died."

The guy set the rifle across his knees and ate, scratching at various places while keeping an eye on us. Liz was adding kindling to the fire and the guy ignored her. She looked at Jamie and me and raised her eyebrows, as if asking permission to act.

Jamie nodded. I saw him tensing his muscles and I slipped my hands out of the cuffs. I knew I wouldn't be able to jump up like Jamie. Whatever was about to play out was going to happen without me. All I could do was administer first aid to whoever was shot, cut, or stabbed.

In what seemed like slow motion, Liz turned sideways, like she planned to pick up another piece of wood. She reached into her back pocket, pulled the Sig pistol out, and held it low, out of sight, looking at it and apparently searching for the safety.

"What're you up to?" The gunman kept his rifle pointed at us but watched Liz.

In a smooth move, she raised the gun, clamped it between her hands, and fired. The guy had a fork full of pasta halfway to his mouth when the bullet hit the bottle of hand sanitizer at his feet. The bullet threw grit into the man's eyes as it burrowed into the ground in front of him. The sanitizer gel erupted from the bottle, spraying his hands, feet, and legs. When the sanitizer splatter reached the fire, the ethanol blazed into a blue flame that raced over everything like napalm.

The guy, partially blinded by the grit, screamed in fear as the blue flames raced over his legs and hands. He rolled away from the fire, his gun thrown aside. Liz backed toward me, keeping the Sig pointed at the screaming man. Jamie bounded toward the guy like a sprinter coming out of the blocks. He had his knife ready to attack, but pulled up short, grabbing the rifle, then kicking dirt onto the last flickering blue flames on the guy's jeans. I had the impression that some of the kicks connected with the shooter's ribs. The blue flames quickly burned out, but his jeans were smoldering. Although the gunman's hands were red, he appeared to be more agitated than injured.

Liz handed me the Sig and started to shake. I put my arm around her and pulled her to me. I felt her arms wrap around me while I pointed the Sig at the ground, watching Jamie pin and then cuff the gunman.

"Lucky shot," I said to Liz.

"That was *not* luck." She pushed herself back from my hug and looking at me indignantly. "I aimed at the sanitizer bottle."

"Really?"

"You told me it was like napalm. I wasn't going to shoot the guy, but I figured if I could get the sanitizer bottle to explode, it'd spew all over him and the fire, and then it would ignite. It was just like shooting a full can of soda pop. Boom! It sprayed all over."

I pulled her into another hug. "You are incredible."

"Are you kidding?" She pulled out of my hug. "That wasn't even a hard shot. It was like all of six feet. Dad and I used to do quick draw with a .45 Colt and shoot cans at ten paces."

"I saw you struggling with the safety and I panicked."

"That was a little dicey. I'm unfamiliar with your pistol and I didn't want to hit the magazine release instead of the safety."

Jamie pulled the guy to his feet, his hands cuffed behind his back. The man's face turned gray and he coughed and gasped for air.

Liz covered her face with her arm. "What's with that cough?"

"What have you been eating," I asked the guy.

"We ate anything I got a shot at. We had ground squirrel one night, jackrabbit, prairie dog, and rattlesnake. Most of the time we went hungry."

"Did Mandy touch any of the dead animals?" I thought about the signs I'd seen posted at Walnut Canyon warning about diseases spread by rodents.

"I'd never actually eaten anything I'd shot before. She said she knew how to skin 'em, so I let her clean the critters while I built a fire to cook them."

Liz watched the guy squirm, trying to itch himself with his elbows. She walked over and lifted his shirttail. "You're covered in flea bites."

"Where've you been sleeping?" Jamie asked.

"Up in one of the buildings at an old mining site. We found some moth-eaten blankets in the bunkhouse and slept on mattresses on the floor."

"Were there lots of mice?" I asked.

"They were around. We could hear them in moving in the walls. I was more worried about a rattlesnake slithering in during the night. We'd seen a couple when we were out hunting."

I checked the safety and slipped the Sig into my waistband. "Get the sat phone, Liz."

She glanced at Jamie's shoulder. "And the first aid kit."

I called Jill's cellphone. "We caught the guy who shot at us."

"Are you all okay?"

"Jamie was hit in the shoulder with a .22. It's a seeping, not a spurting wound. I haven't looked at it, but the bleeding seems to have stopped and he's moving okay. I assume no bones were hit."

"How about you and Liz? Are you two okay?"

"Yes, we're fine, but the guy we arrested has some burns. Liz is putting some kind of salve on his hands."

"How did he get burned?"

"It's a long story. Is the cavalry on the way?"

"The Navajo Nation Police have two vehicles coming to you. Based on the coordinates Liz gave me, I'm guessing we should be there within an hour."

"We?"

"I'm riding with them,"

"I'd hoped for a helicopter evacuation for Jamie and our prisoner."

"You can hope all you want, but the reality is the tribal police caravan is going to be your transport out of there."

"The Grand Canyon has a helicopter."

"I'm not in a position to request assistance from anyone in the Park Service right now,"

"What?"

"I'm in hot water. I don't think anyone in my chain of command would go out of their way to help me out unless camper's lives were at risk. Ray Horn, a Navajo Nation police captain, is very willing to provide assistance."

"Is your problem blowback from something I did?"

"You're still a Park Service hero." Jill gave a brittle laugh. "I have some other issues. Let's leave it at that."

"We found out who the Jane Doe was, and I have an idea what killed her. The guy we have in custody said he was her boyfriend and they were eloping. She got sick, started coughing up blood, and died. The boyfriend is covered with flea bites and has a nasty cough. Call the medical examiner and have him culture for Yersinia pestis and Hanta virus."

"Spell Yersinia for me."

I spelled it out, then added, "Tell him she handled freshly killed ground squirrels, rabbits, and prairie dogs shortly before she got sick and has been sleeping on flea infested bedding in an abandoned mine."

There was a long pause. Then Jill came back. "I radioed Brad and he's calling the M.E. I'm concerned—does this have anything to do with the alert we got about a year ago warning us about plague bacteria in small and medium-sized desert rodents? It specifically mentioned localized plague in prairie dogs and Hanta virus risks in mice."

"My guess is plague. The M.E. and the doctor who'll be testing our detainee will be better able to make that determination."

"Were you exposed?"

"The guy coughed on all three of us."

"Have you been vaccinated against plague? I'm pretty sure I haven't been."

"Plague is bacterial, so we should be treatable with antibiotics. Unless I miss my guess, the guy we arrested will be highly contagious, and at very high risk because it's already gone into his lungs. The first stage of the plague is bubonic, in the lymph system, where the symptoms develop fairly slowly. The second stage is pneumonic. It's highly contagious, is spread through droplets dispersed by coughing, and the patients don't live long without medical treatment."

"There's anthrax here sometimes." Jill said, almost hesitantly. "The spores are in the soil and they get dispersed when the soil is disturbed or when there's a wind storm. The Valley Fever fungus is also endemic in the dust here."

"If it's anthrax, we're in deep trouble and the guy we arrested will be dead before you can get him to a hospital. If it's plague, Valley Fever, or Hanta virus, he's got a chance if he gets to a doctor in time."

"This sounds barbaric, but I'm hoping for plague. It can be treated with antibiotics. Hanta is a virus and Valley Fever is a fungal infection. They're very difficult to treat."

Chapter 14

I'd been focused on Liz and the gunman when I set my wallet and holster behind a rock and hadn't been thinking about identifying landmarks. Now, I walked around somewhat randomly trying to identify a rock or shrub that looked familiar. They all looked remarkably alike. Jamie saw me wandering aimlessly.

"What are you looking for?"

"I set my wallet and holster behind a rock before I walked to the campsite."

He walked over and looked at the ground. "You tried to follow your trail back?"

"What trail? It's all rock and bushes."

He led me back to our footprints. I felt sheepish for not finding and following my backtrail right away. We'd hardly covered ten yards of my trail when I spotted the leather holster behind a large rock. The wallet, with my badge, and ID, were under it.

"Why'd you dump your wallet?" Jamie asked, watching me put the wallet in my back pocket. I pulled the Sig out of my waistband and slipped it into the holster and slid the extra magazine into its slot on the holster.

"The kid didn't know I was a cop. I figured he'd want my wallet and I didn't want him to find my badge."

"You didn't think the pistol and spare magazine would give you away?" Jamie's face was deadpan.

"Hey! It worked, didn't it?"

Jamie shrugged and we walked back to the campsite as I clipped the holster to my belt.

I repacked the gear Liz had dumped from my backpack. Liz opened Jamie's shirt and taped gauze to the top of his shoulder. The tiny bullet hole in his shirt aligned with the gauze on his shoulder.

"Liz patched you up," I said.

"Not much patching required. The bullet grazed me, but didn't create entry and exit wounds, just a gouge. Liz applied antibiotic goo. I told her to put an adhesive dressing on the spot, but she insisted on taping a piece of gauze over it."

Liz had improvised an arm sling from a chunk of fabric despite Jamie's protest he didn't need that kind of support. With Jamie patched up, Liz tended to the gunman's burns.

"I talked to Jill Rickowski. The tribal police should be here in less than an hour."

Jamie examined the sling with disgust. "Good. I'm ready to go home and take a hot shower."

"What about Liz?"

"What about her? She's helping the guy. He has some burns on his hands."

155

"It seemed like you guys hit it off pretty well."

Jamie shrugged.

"Call her when we get back to civilization," I whispered.

"There's no point. She wouldn't like life on the Rez, and I don't want to live in Flag. We'd be at a dead end before we had coffee."

"That's it? Life throws you together, you hit it off, and you're going to walk away."

"I think it's best."

I shook my head. "Neither of you are seeing anyone. You're getting along famously. Call her." I walked away.

* * *

I heard creaking car springs and the scrape of a skid plate dragging across a rock. A cloud of dust drifted down the arroyo and shortly after that two Navajo National Police trucks emerged from the brush.

Captain Ray Horn drove the lead vehicle with Jill in the passenger's seat.

Ray shook my hand while appraising Jamie's sling, bloody shirt, and Liz's field medical care. "What's with you two, Doug? Every time you're teamed up we have a shooting and dead bodies."

"It's good to see you, too, Captain," I said, looking past him at Jill.

"My passenger surprised you?" Ray asked, stepping aside.

"I knew she was coming, although I'm not sure why."

Jill joined our group and shook our hands. "Liz called in and said there were shots fired and you needed backup. You didn't think that'd bring me out?"

"Seems like Captain Horn would have this situation under control and you'd be more important in the office."

"I'm happy to see you even if Doug isn't." Liz hugged Jill.

Liz had extinguished the campfire and cleaned the dishes while Jamie and I were searching for my wallet.

"You sounded pretty rattled on the sat phone, Liz."

"I wasn't sure we'd be seen again when the guy showed up with the rifle. The heroes," she nodded toward Jamie and me, "left me here with nothing to protect myself but a long-handled spoon while they chased the gunshots up on the hill. So, here I am, worried one of them is dying, chewing my nails, and hearing an occasional gunshot. Then this guy comes walking out carrying a rifle and he points it at me."

I shook my head. "Liz is the hero. The guy with the rifle had Liz handcuff us. She got my gun, waited until he was distracted, then disarmed him."

The two tribal police officers who'd arrived in the second SUV were trying hard to load the handcuffed captive into the back seat of their vehicle without getting coughed on. Horn watched them while listening to us.

Horn frowned and turned back toward us. "How did you disarm him, Liz? It looks like he's got some minor burns on his hands. I would've guessed you threw scalding water on him if not for the burns on his jeans."

Liz's hesitancy left the impression she wasn't sure Horn would believe her. "I shot the bottle of hand sanitizer. It blew alcohol all over him and the campfire set it off. I think the flaming alcohol on his hands and legs scared him more than it injured him."

Jill glanced between Jamie and me, checking the validity of Liz's story. We both nodded.

Liz threw up her hands. "Enough with the boys club shit. Jill, won't you accept my story without corroboration from these two?"

Horn rubbed his chin. "You've got to admit it sounds a little far-fetched."

I rose to Liz's defense. "Really. She came up with the plan all by herself. She set him up with the hand sanitizer, chose the timing to make the shot, then hit the bottle squarely on her first and only shot."

Jill went to the campsite garbage bag and pulled out the sanitizer bottle. She examined its ruptured seams and put her finger in the bullet hole, then handed the bottle to Ray Horn.

He turned the bottle in his hand and looked impressed. "I couldn't have hit this bottle exactly in the center like this. That's some good shooting."

Liz smiled. "My dad taught me. I didn't know where Doug's gun was going to shoot so I went for the center of the bottle."

Jill smiled, obviously proud of Liz. "Good aim."

I shook my head. "She didn't aim. Liz swung the gun up like it was an extension of her arm and snapped off the shot when she got centered on the bottle."

"It was just like doing a quick-draw and shooting cans off a fence with a pistol," Liz said.

Horn pulled out an evidence bag from his pocket and dropped the bottle into it. He turned to Liz and offered his hand. "That's better than most of my officers can shoot. Are you interested in law enforcement? I've got a couple retirements coming up."

Liz looked pleased. "I thought you had to be Navajo to serve with you?"

"We've made some exceptions over the years. A woman who shoots like you might be a pretty good addition to the force regardless of your heritage."

Jill raised her hands. "Before you jump to work for Captain Horn, you might want to consider staying with the Park Service. With Doug leaving, I'm down a law enforcement ranger and we can send you to Federal law enforcement training in Georgia if you're interested in law enforcement."

Liz cocked her head and looked at me. "I thought you were back."

"I've taken a posting in Texas. Jill got this investigation set up as temporary duty."

"Would you write a recommendation for me?" she asked.

"I think there are three people standing here who'd all put in a good word for you regardless of which way you decide to go," Jamie said.

Jill nodded toward the truck with the coughing shooter. "Where are you taking the gunman?"

"Tuba City is the closest jail," Horn replied.

"Can he get medical attention there? He sounds like he's in pretty bad shape."

"We'll get him to the clinic."

"Let us know what they find. We may all need to be treated prophylactically with antibiotics because of our exposure to whatever he's coughing up," I said.

Horn nodded. "I'll let you know."

Jill stepped aside and motioned for me to follow her. "Are you okay?" she asked as we walked away from the SUVs.

"I'm fine, just a little achy and tired—nothing a hot shower and a night in a good bed won't repair."

160

I watched Jamie wiggle his arm out of the sling Liz had fashioned for him. He and Horn were having an animated discussion involving Jamie moving his arm around and flexing his elbow and shoulder. It appeared he was pleading his case for returning to duty without going to a doctor.

Jill became serious. "You'll have to continue the search. I talked to the medical examiner and he had already cultured Jane Doe's tissue. In fact, he was unhappy we'd even suggest he wouldn't have already done that as a routine part of the original postmortem. But that's a topic for another day. Anyway, Jane Doe did not die from plague, or anthrax, or any other bacterial or viral infection."

"But the boyfriend said she was coughing up blood, then died."

"Well, that's part of the problem. Jane Doe isn't Mandy Dove. We checked dental records after your call. They don't match. Mandy must be buried out here."

"I don't know what to say. I've been thinking about the shower and the *real* food I was going to eat when we got back to civilization."

"Say you're going to keep looking."

I pulled off my Twins cap, ran my fingers through my sweaty hair, and looked at Liz, who'd joined the discussion with Ray Horn and Jamie. It appeared she had taken Captain Horn's side in the argument that Jamie needed medical care.

"We're kind of burned out after the gunfight and capturing the shooter."

"I hate to be a hard ass, but it'd take a week to gather another team, set them up with supplies, and get them here. You and Liz are already here with several days of food and water. You need to press on. That's what Jamie and Ray Horn are discussing."

"Jamie has a gunshot wound. He needs to see a doctor."

"I hope he'll be able to go on, but we're going to continue either way."

"We, being the royal we, meaning Liz and me?"

"The three of us."

"You're coming with us?"

"I've got a backpack in Ray Horn's SUV."

"You're leaving something unsaid."

"I'd rather not get into that right now." Jill walked away to get her gear, ending the conversation.

I walked over to Liz, Ray, and Jamie, who were standing next to the front of the SUV. "Jill spoke with the medical examiner. They checked dental records and the Jane Doe in the morgue isn't Mandy Dove. He'd also cultured Jane Doe and she didn't die of plague."

Jamie nodded like he already knew. "Captain, do you have a body bag in the SUV?"

Ray went to the back where Jill pulled out a bulging backpack. It had once been bright yellow, but years of use had turned it brown, with the nylon frayed at the corners. It reminded me she'd started out as a ranger, probably guiding hikers as Liz did now. Gone were her polished shoes, replaced with scarred hiking boots looking like they'd been broken in for years. I realized her gray blouse and green pants were lacking the usual military creases I'd seen in the past, replaced with a uniform that had seen a lot of use. She pulled a tattered, wide-brimmed hat from under the pack's flap and put in on her head, then tied a green bandana around her neck. Gone was the office manager, transformed into a backcountry ranger. She left the backpack on the SUV's tailgate and joined us.

Ray Horn removed a black package, about a foot square and several inches thick from the vehicle and handed it to Jamie. I recognized it as a civilian version of a body bag, something I'd seen too often in Iraq. "You think you can find her?" Horn asked.

Jamie nodded. "Liz, can I borrow your shovel?"

"I'm coming along." Liz unstrapped the small shovel and tucked it under her arm. "Which way are we going?"

"You really don't want to do this." Jamie put his hand out for the shovel. "It's going to be unpleasant when we find the body."

"If you guys think I'm good enough to be in law enforcement, then you've got to believe I can handle recovering a dead body. Let's go."

163

"The boyfriend's name is Scott Preston," Jamie said. "If he explained it correctly, his girlfriend's grave is just up the arroyo. She's not buried very deep; he didn't have a shovel."

We'd walked single file up a small arroyo following Jamie, with Jill on his heels. We'd only gone about a hundred yards when Jamie signaled for us to stop. He sniffed the air, then pointed to a spot ahead to our left. He turned his face into the light breeze blowing across the arroyo.

"She's buried over there."

I looked for freshly turned dirt and didn't see anything unusual. "Where?"

"Don't you smell the rotting flesh?"

I shook my head. Liz, carrying the shovel, brought up the rear. She joined us and sniffed the air. "I get a little stink."

Jamie led us up the side of the arroyo to a spot where someone had piled rocks over an area the size of a grave partially hidden by a bush.

"Can you smell it now?"

"Yeah, I've got it now," I replied.

Jill knelt down, picked up some softball-sized rocks covering the grave and set them aside.

Jamie took the shovel from Liz and started pushing smaller rocks. Liz and I picked rocks with Jill. Jamie had scraped down through the dirt half an inch when he uncovered fabric.

Liz grimaced and turned her head. "That smell will gag a maggot."

Jill took the shovel from Jamie, slowly, gently scraping away dirt and revealing the outline of Mandy's body. When most of the body was uncovered, Jill set the shovel aside and pulled blue plastic gloves out of her back pocket and handed each of us a pair. She'd packed a size to fit her hands, so Jamie and I had to stretch ours to get them on. To her credit, Liz hung in there with us, even when the smell became overwhelming. She took a pair of gloves, ready to pitch in.

Jamie loosened a foot in a dirty tennis shoe and lifted it to free the whole leg. The disturbance causing several beetles to skittle away.

Liz recoiled, then watched in silence. "No rigor mortis?"

"Rigor only lasts a couple days," I replied as Jill loosened the girl's arms.

The young woman had been buried in a t-shirt and jeans. With her fingers, Jill gently scraped aside the dirt covering the girl's face. The skin had blackened and started to desiccate, causing it to wrinkle making her look very old. The soil around the mouth started to move and Liz recoiled as dozens of small maggots wiggled in the girl's mouth and nose. She turned away and retched behind me. The stink took me back to autopsies I'd watched while a detective. There hadn't been maggots in the sterile autopsy room at the

Ramsey County Medical Examiners suites, and they had massive fans to suck away the odors. But even there, the stench of a decaying body had been nauseating. Jill flicked the maggots away, unfazed.

Jamie stepped back. "Let's roll her on one side and slide the body bag under her."

"Liz, open the body bag and bring it here." Jill's words brought Liz back to the scene. I heard the rattling of the plastic body bag cover, then Liz reappeared, looking gray, with spittle on the front of her uniform shirt.

"Doug, Jill and I are going to roll the body," Jamie explained. "Liz, I want you to unzip the bag and slide one edge under the body while we have it rolled."

Liz nodded her understanding.

"Now we roll her the other way, into the bag."

"Why don't we just lift her in?" Liz asked.

Jamie looked at Liz and shook his head. "I'm not sure there's enough integrity left in her joints to do that after this much decomposition."

Liz gave that a thought, the implication of his words dawning on her, and she stepped back.

Jamie rolled the legs, Jill lifted the hips, and I rolled the shoulders. When the torso rolled, the left arm flopped leaving it attached, but at an unnatural angle. Jill gently put the pieces in proper orientation. Jamie gathered the two sides of the body bag together over the corpse and zipped the bag closed.

"Jamie, she's facedown." Liz was obviously distressed.

"It doesn't matter. The medical examiner will place her on the exam table when he does the autopsy." Jamie was oblivious to Liz's concern. "Jill, if you and Liz grab the straps at the feet, Doug and I will take the torso straps."

I watched Liz work through her discomfort and steel herself. "She's light," she said as we lifted the bag. The body shifted and sagged, sliding to the center of the black plastic. We backtracked to the SUV.

"I think she'd been nearly starving and some of the body fluids have already leached from the body." Jamie's tone was matter of fact. He'd dealt with dozens of bodies and his approach was totally clinical. Liz struggled with her emotions.

Ray Horn rushed over to help us when we came out of the arroyo. "This is the girlfriend?"

Jamie nodded. "It's a woman and she was buried right where the guy said she'd be."

We loaded the body bag into the back of Ray's SUV and closed the tailgate.

Jamie picked up his pack. "I'm going on with you guys."

Ray Horn shook his head in resignation. "I think you should see a doctor and get some antibiotics."

167

"We'll stay in touch using the sat phone. I'll keep antibiotic cream on the bullet gouge."

"Wait!" I said a second too late, as Jamie slung his backpack onto his shoulders.

Jamie gasped as the strap from the heavy pack bit into the wound. He grabbed the strap and pulled it aside.

Jill pulled the backpack off his shoulders. "Pull out your water and necessities and we'll split them up among Liz, Doug, and me."

Jamie dropped the pack. "If you guys take some of the water I'll be able to handle the rest by hanging the strap on the tip of my shoulder."

"Bullshit." Liz pulled open his backpack. "We've been using water and food out of my pack. I can take most of your gear."

Jamie tried to argue. Liz's glare would've melted ice. "I've got it, Jamie." He stepped back and let her transfer his water and dehydrated food into her pack.

When she was through she looked at Horn. "Captain, can I send our garbage out with you? That'll take a couple pounds out of my pack and make more space."

"Sure." Horn took two small garbage bags from Liz, who used the newly opened space to pack Jamie's water."

I opened a side pocket. "I can take some water, Liz."

"You've barely been able to handle the load you've got, Doug. But if you think you can handle it, take a couple water bottles from Jill to lighten her load. I think her pack only weighs about ten pounds less than she does."

I looked at Jill, who tightened the straps on her pack. She was about five-eight and looked trim. Her pack seemed to be nearly as large as Liz's, meaning it probably weighed forty pounds. She pulled it upright on the SUV's tailgate, turned it so the aluminum frame faced her, then backed up to it, slipping her arms into the straps and hoisting it. She adjusted the straps on her shoulders and pulled the dangling strap across her hips, snapping it with the plastic buckle. She seemed surprised I was watching her when she looked up.

"What?" The weight of the pack didn't seem to affect her.

I lifted up my pack from the ground and struggled to get it on my shoulders. Liz grabbed the shoulder straps and helped me get it balanced. Jill watched with a grin I chose to ignore.

Ray Horn took liter bottles of water out of his SUV and handed one to each of us. "Stay hydrated," he said. Jill drank from her bottle, then poured water over her face, letting it run onto her bandana and blouse. He handed me a blue bandana. "Put this around your neck and keep it moist. It'll help keep you cool."

"Thanks." I tied the bandana around my neck and followed Jill's example, letting the water soak the bandana and the neck of my denim shirt.

169

Chapter 15

Jamie and Liz led the way, with Jill and me following a couple yards behind. Jamie chose the deepest arroyo and set a moderate pace. I hoped I'd be able to keep up.

With Jamie and Liz ahead of us, Jill asked. "What happened back there with the gunman?"

I gave her the brief version of our encounter with the gunman.

"Why did the guy shoot at Jamie?"

"He'd run away with his girlfriend against the wishes of her parents. He apparently saw Jamie's uniform and thought we were a posse sent to find him."

"That's insane."

"Yeah, it wasn't too bright. The guy was covered with flea bites and probably feverish. I don't think he was thinking too clearly."

We walked in silence for half an hour, gaining altitude slowly. The shrubs were greener and a few trees started to appear.

"Why are you here, Jill?"

"Why wouldn't I be? I've got two of my rangers trying to locate the origin of a body that washed onto a national monument."

"It seems like getting daily sat phone reports would be sufficient to keep you informed."

"Don't you want me here?"

"It's not that I don't want you here. I'm just surprised you think this is the best use of your time. I wouldn't expect a park superintendent to strap on a backpack and head out onto the trail."

We walked silently for a few steps while Jill considered her words. "I need to get out of the office once in a while."

"You could take a walk around the visitor center."

"I wanted some fresh air. It's stifling in the office."

"Something came up. You're hiding."

When she didn't reply I looked at her. She stared at the ground and clenched her jaw. She glanced at me and turned her eyes back to the ground.

"Do you want to talk about it?"

"No."

"C'mon. Tell me what you've told your girlfriends."

She stopped walking and turned to me. "I'm married to my job. I'm in my office ten or eleven hours a day, seven days a week. Then I exercise, grab a salad at the store, and go home, eat it in front of the television, then fall into bed exhausted. There are no girlfriends. There's no husband or boyfriend."

"You must socialize."

"I sing in the church choir, but there's no one there who wants to hear about Park Service politics. It's great to get out and even to have coffee afterwards, but there's no one I'd confide in."

"You have a dozen rangers to talk to."

"Doug, they're kids. I have nothing in common with them and they think of me as their intrusive mother. I can't talk with them."

She started walking with determination.

I caught up. "Sorry."

She waved her arm and kept walking.

"I'm not one of the kids. We shared our skeletons when I was in Georgia. Talk to me."

"A hornet's nest got stirred up, that's all."

"Related to what?"

"It's just stupid crap. It'll get sorted out."

"Don't you need to be there to guide the sorting?"

"I think it'll go better if I'm not there. With any luck, it'll all be sorted out when I get back."

"You struck me as someone who wouldn't back away from a fight."

"There's no fight, okay?"

We walked another half hour silently until we saw Jamie and Liz stop and drop their packs. Liz pulled out a water bottle, took a long swallow, then handed it to Jamie. I had a sense Liz's sharing was more than a way of not opening two bottles. I remember childhood arguments about sharing bottles of pop and blaming each other about "back-washing" into the bottle. Liz and Jamie weren't concerned about sharing saliva. I smiled.

Liz was setting up the stove when we reached them. Jamie checked the gauze pad on his wound. I could see the pad was tinged pink, having bled a little when he'd thrown the backpack strap on it. Jill dropped her pack next to Liz's and pulled out a bottle of water. She took a long drink from it and splashed a little water onto her bandana.

"You've got to stay hydrated." She held the bottle out to me.

"We're sharing water bottles?" I set my pack down.

"Do you have a communicable disease I should be concerned about?"

"Not unless I caught the plague from the gunman we arrested."

Jill pulled another bottle out of her pack, making me think maybe she was concerned about catching something from me. A second later she pulled out a dehydrated meal, then handed the water and the food packet to Liz.

"Ah," Liz said, reading the package. "You guys are in for a treat. Jill brought a change of menu. We're having goulash for lunch."

"Sounds good to me." Jamie said, trying to put antibiotic ointment on his own shoulder.

I took the tube from him. "You put a dab of the ointment on the sterile pad, then apply the pad to your wound."

"Why not just squirt some on the gouge?"

"It's not sanitary."

"Doug, it's antibiotic ointment. It kills bacteria. Why worry about contaminating it?"

I taped down the sterile pad. "Nobody wants to use antibiotic ointment contaminated with your blood."

"Doesn't look like anyone but me needs any of it." He pulled his shirt over the bandage. He took the ointment tube and put it into a compartment of his first aid kit, then crumpled the waste and jammed it into his pocket.

Liz heated water and set out plates and cups. I looked around for Jill. I saw a flash of white behind a bush and Jill's hat bobbing above it.

"Nature called," Liz watched my gaze. I nodded my understanding and politely looked away. "There's not much privacy on a backcountry trek."

"Jill is pretty cagey." I squatted next to Liz. "She's the first person to unload water and a meal. RHIP."

"I don't know what that means."

"Rank has its privileges. It's an old Army acronym."

"I hadn't heard that one before," Jamie said, sitting on his backpack. "I always get FUBAR thrown around, mostly in relation to dealing with the FBI."

175

Liz cocked her head. "That's another one I don't know, although I can guess what the 'F' is."

"Fouled up beyond all recognition," Jill said, returning to the group. "We use that acronym in the Park Service too. Liz, do you have some hand sanitizer on top of your pack?"

"I shot the bottle I was carrying."

"Take the one out of my pack, please."

Liz handed the bottle to Jill, who squeezed some onto one hand. She handed the bottle to me. "Want to wash up before lunch?"

I squirted sanitizer on my hand and passed it to Jamie. The aroma of goulash rose from the boiling pot and I realized I was hungry for the first time on the trip.

Liz divided goulash between the plates and handed them out with forks. Jamie dove into his and finished before Jill, Liz, or I were halfway through our portions. He picked up the cookpot and scraped out the inside, eating the last remaining noodles clinging to the sides of the pot and licking off the serving spoon.

"Liz, you can cook for me anytime." He took a tube of lemonade powder and shook it into the remaining water in the bottle he'd shared with Liz. He handed me a tube and I put it into the water bottle between Jill and me.

"Are you sharing that, Doug, or should I make my own lemonade?"

"Do you have any communicable diseases?" I asked. Jill smiled, snatched the bottle from me, and drank from it.

I saw Jamie eyeing the last of the goulash remaining on my plate. I'd been hungry, but Jamie seemed to burn more calories, or maybe had fewer reserves than I did. I handed him the plate and he shoveled the last forkfuls into his mouth.

"Thanks." He scraped the plate with the edge of his fork, then licked the plate clean.

"Would you like a little more?" Jill offered him her plate. She'd eaten about half her portion.

"You don't want any more?" he asked, taking it from her.

"I'm not a big fan of dehydrated food." She opened the flap of her backpack and pulled out a plastic bag filled with trail mix. She took a handful and passed the bag to me. "Want some gorp?"

"Gorp?" I asked, shaking the trail mix into my hand.

Liz said, shook a handful of trail mix into her hand. "Good old raisins and peanuts."

"I fortified it with candy," Jill said.

Jamie set aside Jill's cleaned plate and poured trail mix into his hand. "You Park Service guys eat well. I live on power bars and water when I'm hiking by myself. This is gourmet eating compared to most of my hikes." He handed the bag back to Jill, who squeezed the air out and resealed the zipper before stowing it.

"I like cooking for Jamie." Liz put the stove in her backpack. "He appreciates the food and there aren't any leftovers or garbage when he's done."

Jamie smiled. "My pleasure." He drank more lemonade and handed the bottle to Liz.

Jill nudged me and she handed our shared bottle back. "Finish it up. Dehydration kills." I drank the last and then crushed the bottle into a flat piece that Jill slipped into her backpack.

Jamie unfolded a map and spread it on the ground while Liz sanitized the plates. He put his finger on a spot not far east of the riverbed.

"We're about here. I figure there's another four or five miles of this arroyo before we hit this ravine cut into the hillside. If we don't find something before we get very far into the ravine, we're done. I don't think there would have been enough flow to carry a body above that spot."

Jill nodded. "We should be there before dark."

Jamie folded the map. "If we don't break again to eat."

"Let's just push on and we'll eat where we're going to camp," Jill looked at me. "Will your knee hold up if we push a little harder?"

"It's fine," I lied. Climbing through hills after the gunman and the fall had my knee aching. Another four or five miles would be torture.

"Let's go!" Liz secured the flap on her backpack.

Jill struggled to get her pack off the ground. I gave her a hand, then she helped me. Jamie and Liz watched in amusement.

"You guys need a walker or wheelchair?" Jamie asked.

Jill gave him a go away gesture. "We've got it. Get going. We'll be right behind you."

It didn't take long for Jamie and Liz to get far enough ahead so they were out of our sight.

"I get tired of the old lady humor."

"Do you get a lot of that?"

"Not a lot, at least not to my face. I hear the comments about 'mother' and 'grandma' when the young rangers don't know I'm around."

"Sounds like age discrimination."

"It's not that. It's just . . . I'm closer to their parents' age than I am to theirs. They wander around listening to rap music and texting on their smartphones. I'm always the bad guy who reminds them they're on duty, that they have to be professional all the time, not just when they know someone is watching. A lot of them don't *get* that they are the face of the Park Service and when they look or act inappropriately, they reflect on all of us."

"It's a different world from the one we grew up in."

"I spend a lot of time reminding them that when they're wearing the uniform they need to act like professionals."

"Most of them have never been in the military. That gets beaten into you pretty well during basic training, no matter which branch of the service you've served in."

"I think part of it is their parents. The young rangers are a cross-section of society. In some respects, we're getting the cream, because they're virtually all college graduates. But lots of them come from families with divorces, single moms, non-custodial fathers, and more. Their parents have tried, but their own lives are fragmented and over stressed. There were no stay-at-home moms, and if anything, they come from families where both parents were overachievers, working sixty hours a week."

"Like you."

"Like me. But I'm not trying to raise a kid."

I tripped over a rock and pitched sideways into Jill. She saw me stagger and anticipated my movement, getting her arm out to steady me before I knocked both of us to the ground.

"Thanks." I readjusted my pack and let the adrenaline dissipate.

Jill pulled out a water bottle and took a drink, then poured some over her face. It soaked her bandana. She handed the bottle to me. "Here. Hydrate."

I took a drink and tried pouring water over my face. Most ran down my shirt.

"Keep your bandana moist. It'll help keep your head cooler."

"Okay. I'm ready."

Jill set a moderate pace, which probably meant Jamie and Liz were getting farther ahead by the minute. Jill seemed unconcerned.

I watched Jill striding effortlessly under the weight of her pack. "You're strong."

"Is that a compliment?"

"Yes."

"I spent years being called a tomboy."

"You've made your mark in a field dominated by men. You've got to be emotionally strong and resilient, and that's not being a tomboy."

She considered my words without comment.

"But you're physically strong too. A lot of women washed out of National Guard basic training because they couldn't handle a heavy backpack and the physical challenges. And you're a couple years older than those girls, who were in their prime."

"You were doing well until you added the age qualifier."

Not knowing how to extricate my foot from my mouth, I shut up.

"Did I hurt your feelings?" she asked after a few minutes.

"I was trying to be polite, then suddenly tasted my foot. I figured I'd quit digging myself in deeper."

Jill turned her head and smiled. "You really can't tell when I'm kidding."

"Apparently not."

"The Eagles or AC/DC?" she asked.

"What?"

"Do you prefer The Eagles, or do you listen to AC/DC?"

"I'm more of an Eagles guy. How about you?"

"I grew up with *Hee Haw* reruns on television and Country Western music on the car radio. The Eagles were a big jump for me, and about as hard rock as my parents would tolerate."

"I wasn't a lot into music. I played football and was in Scouts. I remember going to school dances and standing in a corner with all the other introverts who didn't know music and were afraid to talk to a girl."

"You were afraid to talk to girls?"

"Terrified. I asked a girl to the prom junior year and she said, 'no.' I was so embarrassed I didn't go on a date until Martha Stiles asked me to the Sadie Hawkins dance when I was a senior."

"What's a Sadie Hawkins dance?"

"The girls ask the guys."

"So, was Martha the first great love of your life?"

"Oh God, no." I laughed. "She was a friend from the neighborhood who took pity on me. We went on a movie date once after the dance, but it was too stressful. I tried to kiss her goodnight, but I started shaking. She laughed, pecked me on the cheek, and went inside without saying goodnight.

"How about you? Did you have a great high school romance?"

"The boys were afraid of me. I played Little League with them and I could outrun, out hit, and out field any guy on the team. I went through school with the same bunch of guys I'd embarrassed in grade school and they never forgave me. I was always the tomboy. I heard some whispers I was a lesbian and that was the social kiss of death in small-town South Dakota."

I had no response, not wanting to ask the obvious question.

"I'm not a lesbian. That's the question you were afraid to ask, right?"

"I figured it wasn't any of my business."

"You were being politically correct. I know. I took the training, too."

"So, off to college, and all the repressed sexuality was suddenly unleashed," I joked.

"Hardly. Nobody was interested in asking out the flat-chested nerd who dressed in western-cut shirts, blue jeans, and cowboy boots. I hid in the library and made myself into the complete hermit nerd."

"And then you got a job with the Park Service."

"Yes, and then I joined the Park Service. You mentioned the National Guard. Was that your first step after high school?"

"My dad died, and I didn't know what to do with myself. We'd always talked about going to college, but there wasn't money for tuition anymore. I joined the Guard, went to summer camp, and tried to figure out what to do with myself."

"And you came home from summer camp and joined the police?"

"That wasn't even on the radar. I got a job at a grocery store and started taking some general education classes at a junior college. I went to my monthly Guard meetings and, at some point, a counselor at the college suggested I take a criminal justice class and transfer to his military police National Guard unit. They were under their numbers, and I'm sure his interest was totally self-serving, but I made the switch and I liked it."

"Can you reach a water bottle in the side pocket of my backpack?"

We stopped and I pulled the bottle out. We both drank.

"You're helping me do a better job of staying hydrated," I said. "Let's take a break and I'll go water some bushes."

"You guys have it so easy," she said with a laugh. "All you have to do is pull down a zipper and you've got relief. I see a modesty bush right over here."

We set our packs down on the hardpacked arroyo dirt.

"Men right and women left," Jill said.

I nodded my understanding and moved to the bushes on the right side of the trail. After pulling up my zipper, I turned around and realized the 'modesty bush' Jill had chosen didn't reach all the way to the ground. Jill attempted modesty, but her white granny panties were resting on top of her uniform pants and boots, with a pair of white ankles above them.

Jill, you don't get much sun working sixty hours a week, I thought to myself. I saw her hands grab the panties and pants and heard the rattle of a buckle. I turned back toward a bush and pretended to be zipping up.

After rubbing sanitizer over our hands, we helped each other into the backpack straps and started back up the arroyo.

"If you're working sixty hours a week, how do you stay in shape? No desk jockey is going to be able to heft that backpack."

"I go from work to the gym. It serves a dual purpose: I get exercise and I take out my aggressions and frustrations in a constructive way."

185

"Rather than beating on the furniture and throwing things?"

"More like not telling some Washington bureaucrat to go suck an egg when he calls to tell me to take another two percent out of my budget or when one of the female rangers comes into my office in tears to tell me she got a 'Dear John' letter telling her the boyfriend is screwing her best friend, 'sniffle', and John isn't answering her phone calls, 'sniffle', and if he'd only talk to her, 'sniffle', she's sure she'd be able to explain the error of his ways, 'double sniffle.' Sometimes I'd just like to say, 'Listen sister. If he's sleeping with your best friend, he's not worth keeping.'"

"That's not what you say?"

"Oh, hell no. I play mom. I hug them and let them cry on my shoulder while murmuring soft reassurances like, 'Things will be better. There are more fish in the sea. He doesn't deserve someone as sweet and kind as you.'"

"Does any of that work?"

"Ultimately, no. But it turns off the tears and gets them out of my office."

"Your job sucks."

Jill laughed, displaying dimples. "I love about seventy-five percent of it and don't mind about twenty percent of it. But yes, there's five percent that pretty much sucks."

"Your whole life is the job and the gym?"

"There's more," she said defensively.

186

"Like what?"

"I told you I sing in the church choir."

"Really? You're like the mezzo soprano?"

"I'm like the alto who sings softly and hides in the second row. I used to sing in the high school choir, and I met the Presbyterian church choir director at a grocery store after a Sunday service. We got talking and I told her how much I'd enjoyed listening to the choir. She asked if I'd ever sung, then invited me to the next choir practice. Suddenly, I was committed to choir practice every Wednesday night, followed by coffee and conversation at a coffee shop, and two Sunday services."

"Sounds like a nice diversion from the office."

"It is. I can totally empty my mind and focus on the harmonies. Plus, there's a lot of camaraderie among the choir members, and the Wednesday evening gab sessions at the coffee shop are a hoot. There's lots of laughter, some gossip, and some church politics. As soon as the politics come up, I'm out of there." We walked in silence through a rocky area where we focused on not twisting an ankle. Then Jill asked, "How about you? What do you do with your days off?"

"Not much. I haven't connected with anyone here. The other rangers are either too young or married with children. I went to a couple bars, but I'm not really into drinking anymore, and the women I met were bar flies who drank way too much, or they were ditzy and superficial. So, I gave up on that scene. Mostly, I watch television, wash laundry, ride my bike, and read the newspaper."

"Do you have any family back in Minnesota?"

"My mother's still alive and we used to talk regularly, but we've drifted apart. She wasn't pleased I was a cop and she was more displeased when I divorced her delightful, college professor daughter-in-law. Mom thought my ex-wife walked on water. Other than that, there are a bunch of aunts, uncles, and cousins who've drifted away. You met my cousin, Eleanor, when she and her husband were down last summer. I email El, and they're planning another Flagstaff trip this winter when the Snowbowl is open for snowboarding."

"There's Sheila," Jill said, smiling.

"Yeah, there's Sheila."

"She seems perky and interested in you."

"She's perky and pesty. I feel like she's more interested in a daddy for her two boys than she is in me, and I'm not up for a ready-made family. Nor am I interested in someone who spends as much time in front of a mirror as Sheila does. Her hair and makeup are always perfect, and she dresses in carefully coordinated outfits. I prefer my women a little more wash and wear."

"What's a wash and wear woman?"

"I suppose she's like my cousin El. Someone who hops into the shower, dries off, and is ready to move on with her day with damp hair and no makeup."

"As I recall, El had short, straight hair, and a Scandinavian complexion that didn't need makeup."

"I think it's more about being comfortable in your own skin than having a perfect complexion. You do a good job of that."

"I'll take that as a compliment."

"You radiate self-confidence. My experience is women get picked on and bullied over their clothing and appearance until all their self-confidence is stripped away."

"And I guess I'm also wash and wear."

She stopped abruptly and grabbed my arm. I looked at the hand gripping my forearm firmly and felt her pulling me back. I looked up and saw her fixated on the trail in front of us. Then I heard the rattle.

"Snake," she whispered, continuing to pull me back.

Adrenaline flooded my system as Jill pulled me. I tripped on a rock and nearly fell as I drew my pistol and backpedaled.

"You could've yelled, 'snake!'"

We watched in silence as the brown and black body slithered across the trail.

"I couldn't."

"Why not? Were you afraid you'd scare the snake?" I asked as the adrenaline ebbed from my bloodstream.

Jill bent over and put her hands on her knees, taking deep breaths. "I couldn't yell."

"Why?" I asked, slipping the Sig back into the holster.

Jill glared at me. "Because I was scared shitless. You're lucky I said 'snake' and grabbed your arm. We were within its striking distance." Jill pulled a water bottle out of her pack and took a drink, then handed it to me. "Did you even see it before I pulled you back?"

"No." I realized I'd been ignoring the trail and consumed in our conversation. "I'm not up on my snake bite first aid. I've heard that sucking out the venom isn't an appropriate response anymore."

"No. The only effective treatment is getting the victim to an emergency room for anti-venin injections."

"We're a long way from a hospital. Would I die from the snake bite before transport could get me to an E.R.?"

"Depends on where you're bitten. If you're hit in the fleshy part of an extremity, you're not likely to die, but you're going to have some major tissue damage as the venom attacks. If you're hit in the head, or if a fang goes into a major blood vessel, you might die. Either way, it's going to be an unpleasant experience."

"Is a snake bite the greatest threat on the trail?"

190

"That and falling into an old mine pit. There are tens of thousands of old mines in the hills and one or two people a year fall into them."

"Don't the mines have to close the openings to their shafts?"

"Now they do, but 'back in the day' the miners just walked away when the ore vein ran out. Who knows, maybe we'll stumble into the Lost Dutchman mine."

"Is that around here?" I asked, scanning the hills.

"Doug, it's called the 'Lost Dutchman' because no one knows where it is. Hence the adjective, Lost." Jill paused. "It's generally thought to be in the Superstitions south of here."

Jamie appeared on the trail ahead of us, interrupting the discussion. He stopped and let us catch up.

"What's up?" Jill asked.

"Nothing. Liz just asked me where you were, and I said I didn't know. I came back to make sure you hadn't turned up the wrong arroyo somewhere."

Jill shook her head. "We've been following your tracks. We're just slow."

I felt a sudden pang of guilt. I hadn't been following their tracks, having been too distracted by my pleasant discussion with Jill.

Jamie fell in step beside us. "We're just about to the end of the arroyo and I haven't seen anywhere that looks like a body washed out of it."

"Have we passed any branches large enough to have been carried in a significant flash flood flow?"

"I don't think so. If we don't find something by the time we get to the ravine, I might rethink that, but I haven't seen anything that made me want to follow a different arroyo yet, and they're getting smaller."

Jill glanced at me. "Maybe this isn't where Jane Doe came from."

"I guess we'll have to discuss our options over a campfire tonight."

Chapter 16

Liz was lying on a patch of dried grass with her headscarf pulled over her eyes. She looked very contented and she made me wish I could take a nap.

"Sleepyhead! I found them."

Liz pushed her headscarf up with one finger and turned to look at us. She made no move to get up.

Jill looked around. "Is this where we're spending the night?"

"Jamie wants to go another half mile, but his pack probably only weighs two pounds. I'm willing to crash right here." She rolled up onto one elbow. "What do you guys think?"

Jill looked at me.

"I'm the wrong person to ask. I was ready to climb in the SUV and ride back to Tuba City with Ray Horn."

Jamie pled his case. "In half a mile we'll be out of arroyo, and if we haven't found anything, we can either come up with plan B, or we can hike back out."

"I've got a different Plan B," said Liz. "You trot ahead and check out the next half mile while we set up camp here and I cook supper. When you get back, we'll eat and then decide what to do."

Jamie looked at me, then gave a nod of resignation. "I'll be back in a while."

Jill and I helped each other lower our packs to the ground. Liz watched Jamie disappear down the arroyo at nearly a trot.

"You two look like it'd kill you to walk another twenty yards," Liz said after making sure Jamie was gone. "I could've gone on, but I think you guys should crash."

"Jamie seemed to have energy left over."

"I've been trying to slow him down all day. He's not human. I mean he has one speed that's nearly a trot. I swear he can keep it up all day long like a marathon runner."

Jill sat down next to Liz like her legs had given out. She flopped on her back with her knees in the air. "Doug, I didn't tell you this when you started this expedition, but Liz is my most experienced backcountry guide. She does a fabulous job of tailoring her hikes to the hikers. If she's got mountain men, she has them trucking along at a lope. When she has more senior or junior hikers, she slows the pace. In each case, the groups feel like she's given them the perfect experience."

Liz smiled. Unable to take the praise, she busied herself by pulling out the camp stove and cookware.

"In our case, I think she has determined we've hit the wall and it is time to have us dump our packs and take a break."

"I'd say she read me pretty well." I sat next to Jill.

"Have you ever been this far onto the reservation, Liz?" Jill asked.

"My trips always end on Park Service land, somewhere south of where you joined us. None of this is familiar to me." Liz pulled a liter of water out of each of our packs and set a pot on the stove.

"Bless you," I said.

"What?" Liz asked as she poured water into the pan.

"I'm thanking you for taking some water out of my pack. I'd be willing to give up more if you need it."

Liz laughed. "I'll take bids after supper. Highest bidder gets to take out two liters of water."

I nodded. "I'm ready to trim the handle on my toothbrush to lighten the load,"

"Yeah, we've joked about trimming the margin off the maps to lighten them. The hard part is the water. It's the heaviest thing we pack, and it's the most necessary. If we don't bring a gallon a day per person, we're risking dehydration and heat stroke."

Liz held up two packages. "Chili or beans and rice for supper?"

I groaned.

"I take it you aren't a fan of the freeze-dried chili?"

"So far, it's the worst of the bad options."

195

Liz returned the chili to her backpack. "Jamie liked it. He ate all the leftovers."

"Jamie's eaten all the leftovers from every meal. He's no connoisseur."

"Would you prefer pasta primavera?" Liz asked.

"Just throw something in the pot. Call it chef's surprise because we'll all be surprised if it's edible."

"They're calories you'll need to keep going. You should've eaten the last of your goulash instead of giving it to Jamie," Liz said.

"Jamie hasn't got any fat reserves, and he moves around like a water bug. He's burning more calories sitting still than I burn moving."

Jill sat up abruptly and untucked her shirt. She unbuttoned two buttons and flapped her shirt as she threw off her hat. I looked at her to see if she was having a seizure or something medically acute was happening.

"You okay?" I asked.

"Sorry. I'm having a hot flash. It'll go away in a couple minutes. Then I'll be cold." I could see the sheen of sweat on her brow and arms as her body reacted to the hot flash. I grabbed a bottle of water from my backpack and handed it to her. She doused her head with some, then took a drink. "Thanks."

Liz dumped the packet of beans and rice into the boiling pot and stirred. While it cooked, she pulled out more tubes of flavoring for the water. "How about raspberry iced tea for supper."

Jill continued flapping her shirt. "Sounds lovely. Put extra ice in mine." She unbuttoned the remaining shirt buttons and flapped it more vigorously. The flapping uncovered her flat stomach and sports bra. She was lean and muscular. The sports bra pressed her small breasts against her chest.

"My eyes are up here," she said, catching me staring at her torso. Embarrassed, I quickly looked up and saw her smiling. "Camping is one of those activities where you have to check your modesty at the trailhead. Everyone is dealing with normal body functions and this cover doesn't provide a lot of privacy when you've got your pants around your ankles."

Jill suddenly buttoning up. "Hot flash is over and now we're into the rebound. You men have it so easy. You zip and unzip to pee, you don't start a menstrual period when you're at the furthest point from the trailhead or other services, and no hot flashes. It's all easy for you."

"Twice as many male rangers die a year as female rangers," I said. "Tell me again how we male rangers have it so easy."

"That's because men take stupid chances. Most deaths are due to falls, followed by animal attacks. Female rangers have the foresight to anticipate some of those things."

Jamie trotted back to camp. "There's a sweat lodge just up the ravine."

Jill responded to my vacant look. "It's like a Navajo sauna."

"Supper is ready," Liz announced. She started scooping steaming portions onto the aluminum plates.

Jamie looked annoyed. "It's leaning into the arroyo. It might be the source of the body. Let's go."

"Is there anyone around?" Jill stood.

"Not at the moment."

Liz held out a plate to him. "Then eat. It'll still be undisturbed after supper."

Jamie looked annoyed but took a plate and sat down. Jill took plates for us and sat next to me.

"Raspberry iced tea." Liz handed a tube to Jill and took another for herself. Jill and Liz poured the dry flavoring into their water bottles and shook.

"Tell us about the sweat lodge," Jill suggested, taking a bite of beans and rice

"It's built in a little aspen grove by a spring," Jamie said between bites. "There's a tarp on top, and the bent branch support structure is holding up the dome. It's sitting on the edge of the arroyo and the flash flood undercut it, so part of it is right at the edge of the cut bank."

"What's the significance? It's just a sauna," I said.

Jamie waved his fork and shook his head while he chewed and swallowed. "A sweat lodge is more than just a sauna. Sweat lodge ceremonies are like Catholic sacraments. They can only be conducted by an elder, and the participants are looking for a vision or a change in their lives."

Liz waved a spoonful of beans and rice. "It also means there've been people up here. We haven't seen much of anything for miles."

Jamie finished his dinner and glanced at our plates, apparently hoping someone wouldn't want all their meal. I was a little more than half done and wasn't enamored with the meal. I handed him my plate and he dove into it.

"You're not eating enough calories. We're burning more than we're getting from full portions," Liz said to me.

"I've got fat reserves," I patted my stomach. "I'd be happy to shed a couple pounds."

Jill opened her pack and handed me the trail mix. "Have some. It'll give you a jolt of energy."

I took a handful and set the bag on the ground where the others could reach it. Jamie, having cleaned both his and my plates, took a handful of trail mix and popped some in his mouth.

Jill scraped her plate. "There have been a couple of newspaper articles about self-proclaimed medicine men doing sweat lodge healing ceremonies. They're amateur healers and they've been chased out of a couple towns in

Utah and New Mexico after the police started getting reports about people being rushed to the hospital for heat stroke and smoke inhalation."

"A real sweat lodge ceremony is conducted by an elder," Jamie explained. "They train as apprentices for at least four years before being allowed to conduct their own sweats, and it's more than just a sauna. There's smudging with sage, then drums and chanting. Inside the lodge an elder passes a pipe and each participant bows to the four compass directions and takes a puff of tobacco. There's no fire inside the lodge, only heated rocks, so no smoke inhalation. There's more too, but I don't remember it all. I was pretty young the last time I saw a real sweat ceremony."

I took another handful of trail mix. "For every naïve person, there's a charlatan ready to bilk them. There were a couple in Minnesota doing sweat ceremonies, but they were more a way to bond the members more closely, leading to 'initiation' of the young women. One cult leader was chased down in Central America and brought back. He pled guilty to having sex with minors and will probably be beaten to death in prison if the rest of the prisoners ever find out who he really is."

"Liz, can you hand me the sat phone?" Jill asked. Liz dug in her backpack and pulled it out. Jill walked away from the group while the phone powered up. She punched in a number from memory and walked farther away.

"Well, Jamie, shall we find some firewood while Liz cleans up the dishes?"

He stood and waited for me to go slowly from sitting, to kneeling, to standing "Are you sure you want to do this? I can get firewood and you can stay sitting, or maybe lying down."

"I've got to move or my knees will lock up." I hobbled along behind him.

We roved through the bushes and low trees, picking up brush and occasionally breaking a dead branch off a tree. Jamie did most of the picking and I carried the growing pile of kindling.

Jamie quickly had an armload of wood. "There's a lot more fire material here than on Park Service land. I suppose every group of campers is scavenging wood down there. We may be the only humans who've walked this area in a couple hundred years."

"I thought prospectors combed this area for uranium during the cold war," I said.

"You're right. There were dozens of people trekking the hills, breaking rocks, and digging, in hopes of finding ore deposits. They certainly came through here."

"I wonder what kind of a deal the government had with the tribe to allow prospecting on the reservation?"

"You're joking," said Jamie. "It's just like the South Dakota Black Hills gold rush. The government gave the tribes land they thought was worthless. As soon as there's an ore discovery, the treaties are reinterpreted, and the sovereignty of the reservation isn't as important as white men making money off the ore."

"I never read about the uranium mining down here," I said.

"That's because white historians wrote the history books," Jamie picked up two large limbs broken from a tree and decided they were too much for me. "I think we've got plenty of wood for tonight."

"Tell me about the sweat lodges."

"A traditional lodge is like an igloo made over a frame of bent saplings. There's a small opening on one side, just large enough to crawl through, and it's covered with grass and whatever can be found nearby. Then there are blankets thrown over the top to seal in the heat better."

"Rocks provides the heat?"

"Yes. There's a big fire outside where rocks are heated. Once everyone is seated inside, a fire starter carries seven hot rocks into the lodge using deer antlers and puts them in a hole in the center of the lodge. He closes the door when he leaves, and the elder puts water on the rocks to create steam. The fire starter refreshes the rocks three times and checks with the elder to see if anyone needs to leave. It's bad form to get sick and leave between the rock deliveries because the tradition dictates the door only be opened four times and if someone leaves early, it breaks the sweat and the elder has to decide whether they go on, or whether they bring everyone out and call the ceremony off."

"It sounds complicated."

"It is. I only covered the high points. It takes years for an elder to be trained to lead a sweat, and I'm not well versed in all the traditions."

"Why would a ceremony be held out here? This is in the middle of nowhere."

Jamie walked silently beside me for a while, then said. "There's no reason to build a lodge out here. Sweats are done away from town, but not in the middle of nowhere."

"So, what's close?"

"I'll look at the map when we get back to camp. I think the closest access point is probably an old mining road running through the ranch and abutting the reservation."

I stopped. "If that's the case, the lodge wasn't built by your people."

"It's not likely," Jamie replied as he resumed walking.

"We may be dealing with the bogus medicine man Jill mentioned."

"Or someone like him."

"Will you be able to tell by looking at the lodge?"

"I was already suspicious. The tarp over the lodge is plastic, the kind you'd buy at Walmart or Home Depot. My people use blankets or canvas. I'll bet they used wire to secure the saplings, too. Tradition dictates the saplings be tied with natural material, like tree bark or sometimes twine."

We walked into camp where Liz and Jill were sitting side by side sipping from aluminum cups. A steaming aluminum pot sat on the stove. I caught the aroma of coffee and started to salivate. I dumped my accumulation of branches on a bare spot a few feet away from the cooking area, and Jamie immediately started assembling the kindling for a fire.

"Coffee?" Liz asked.

She didn't wait for my answer and started pouring a cup for me. I sat next to Jill and accepted the cup from Liz. The aluminum was so hot I had to carefully hold the handle and set the cup on the fabric of my pants while I waited for it to cool.

"Jamie says the sweat lodge isn't a Navajo design. They used a plastic tarp on top and I guess that's not kosher."

Jill cocked her head. "Kosher?"

"I don't know the right word," I backpedaled, feeling sheepish. "It's not the prescribed material for a Navajo sweat ceremony. Is that better?"

Liz laughed and Jill smiled. I rolled my eyes at once again being the butt of a joke. The tinder started to crackle, and Jamie added larger pieces of wood to the fire.

Liz leaned close to Jill and whispered, "He's better at campcraft than anyone I've ever seen. I'm in awe."

Jamie must've heard her, because he looked up and smiled.

"What did the Park Service have to say, Jill?" I took a tentative sip of coffee and discovered it was still too hot to drink."

"The bigshots are interviewing everyone and reading personnel files." She glanced at Liz, then added, "I can't really say any more."

"Is there really that much drama between the rangers, Liz?"

"It's not everyone. We're kind of a starter posting, where a lot of people start out as seasonal hires, then move on to permanent jobs in prestigious parks if they do okay and decide to stay with the Park Service."

"You've met the young rangers who live in the trailers," Jill said. "They're the newbies and the trailers sometimes get to be drama scenes. There are young men mixing with young women and sparks of romance flare and die out. I sometimes get dragged in to mediate. Other times the people sort it out themselves or they leave, either to another park, or for home."

"I'm spoiled by the people like Brad and Liz, who've been here years and provide the continuity to keep things operating smoothly and keep me sane. They do their jobs without drama and come to me with solutions rather than problems." Jill reached out and patted Liz on the knee. "I don't tell you often enough how much I appreciate you."

"I love you too, Mom," Liz had an evil grin. She raised her eyebrows at me and added, "Jill hates being called Mom."

Jamie, smelling of smoke, sat beside Liz. "Any more coffee?"

"Sure." Liz pulled another cup from her backpack and poured for Jamie while he dug in his backpack for something.

Producing two candy bars, he handed one to Jill. "It's all I've got left, but half a candy bar and a cup of coffee will make a pretty nice bedtime snack." He peeled open his bar and broke off half, handing it to Liz.

Jill handed me the half still in the wrapper. She bit into her half and closed her eyes. "Mmm."

I chewed a bite of candy and washed it down with tepid coffee. "That's a pretty nice camp dessert."

I watched Jill lick the chocolate from her fingers. It looked sensual. She felt my eyes on her, glancing at me while she still had a finger in her mouth. I think she read my mind because red started to creep up her face. She quickly looked away. She pulled a tissue from her pocket and wiped off the last of the chocolate, then threw the tissue into the fire.

She made a quick segue. "So, Jamie, the sweat lodge isn't Navajo?"

"I told Doug the Dine', the Navajo people, don't use plastic tarps on sweat lodges. That, and we're not near any Navajo settlements or residences." He pulled the dog-eared map out of his backpack and unfolded it in the dying twilight. He placed his finger on a location near the edge of the reservation.

"We're here." He pointed west, off the reservation. "The nearest road is here, on the abutting ranch. I think that's where the builders came from. They're roughly copying the Native design, but not exactly. I'm guessing we've got someone putting on sweat ceremonies for tourists."

Jill considered Jamie's comments. "The medical examiner hasn't been able to determine Jane Doe's cause of death. A lot of that may be due to decomposition and the damage done by scavengers. The lack of trauma to the body could be consistent with a number of things, including heat stroke during a sweat ceremony."

"What was she wearing?" Jamie asked.

"She was in a beaded buckskin dress. I assume that's something traditional."

Jamie shook his head. "Someone wants you to think traditional dress was associated with this, but the elders and sweat participants all wear light cotton clothes. The men are in white cotton pants. The women wear homemade white cotton dresses. You want to wear something that'll soak up the sweat."

"Please hand me the sat phone again, Liz," Jill pushed the power button on the phone and waited for it to warm up and connect with the satellites. We all watched in silence.

She entered a phone number from memory and waited. "Brad, it's Jill again. We've been talking, and the sweat lodge Jamie found is not Navajo. Do a search, online and newspapers, to see if you can find anything about someone claiming to be a medicine man, or spiritual leader who's conducting sweat ceremonies near Flagstaff." Jill listened for a few more moments, then disconnected and shut down the phone.

"And?" I asked.

"I talked to Brad Peck, the lead ranger at Walnut Canyon. He's going to do some research. He didn't know of anything like that going on locally, but he's going to see what the internet may have. I'll check back with him at noon tomorrow and see what he's found."

Jamie got up and added the largest branches to the dying fire. We all scooted closer and watched the flames lick at the new logs as they popped and shot tiny embers into the air.

"Did anyone bring the makings for S'mores?" Silence followed Jill's question. "I've never been on one of your backpack trips, Liz. What do you do in the evenings?"

"We watch the fire. If I've got kids along I tell ghost and Bigfoot stories. If it's just adults, we sit around and talk."

I took a sip of coffee that had gone from too hot, to tepid, to cool, in the time we'd been talking. "No singing 'Kumbaya'?"

"Not usually. I've had a couple church and Girl Scout groups and they sang, but I don't offer that up. I'm not much of a singer."

I smiled at Jill who shook her head and frowned. She mouthed, "No."

Jill quickly turned away. "Jamie, what's your plan for tomorrow?"

"I'm going to check out the sweat lodge and the area around it to see who's been there and what they might've left behind. I'm hoping it's seen some regular use so there's a trail we can follow to see where the people have been walking."

"You said it had been undercut by the flash flood. That must mean it hasn't been used since the flood. There won't be any footprints to follow," I said.

"It's still out of the arroyo, just on the edge of the cut bank. You don't need footprints to follow a trail. If a few people have been through there'll be matted grass and broken twigs on the bushes. I'm sure I can follow their backtrail.

We watched the fire die to embers and then the embers became glowing ashes. Liz got up and kicked dirt over the ashes.

"When I was in Scouts, we always drowned a fire," I said, getting up slowly. My muscles had stiffened.

"Water's precious out here," Liz replied. "We bury the embers."

"Nobody ever gets a hotfoot wandering around in the dark?"

"Not so far. I suppose you could be the first."

The half moon cast enough light for me to unstrap my bedroll and find a flat spot without rocks to spread it. I must've made a good choice because the others joined me in a fairly small area.

Liz pulled out her bedroll. "Everyone's sleeping under the stars so I don't need to break out the tent?"

"Not for me." Jamie threw out his mat and blanket, and we all arranged ourselves side-by-side. I had socks under my head for a pillow. I watched Jill pull out a small package and blow up an inflatable pillow. I must've given her a strange look because she asked, "What"

"An inflatable pillow seems like an extravagance."

"Not if you've been thrown from a horse and have neck issues."

I struggled to get the foam pad flat, then get myself on top of it before it recoiled. Jill, lying next to me, watched with amusement. Finally settled, I had to pee. Crawling out from under the blanket, I got to my feet.

"Nature calling?" Jill turned on a small penlight and held it out to me. "Don't step in the hot embers or kill yourself tripping over a rock."

When I returned, I shut off the light and handed it back to her. "I think it's the coffee. I don't usually have any diuretic liquids this late in the day."

She slid the flashlight under her pillow. "I'm buzzing from the caffeine."

I got the bedroll situated and was lying there awake, regretting the caffeine after supper. I stared at the sky and the Milky Way. There were a billion visible stars, probably ten times as many as I could see from my townhouse among the streetlights and houses. A coyote howled and a second joined in, slightly out of synch.

I flinched and reached for the Sig when a hand grabbed the blanket in the middle of my chest. I relaxed when I realized Jill's hand was clutching my blanket. I rolled toward her and saw fear in her eyes.

"What?"

"I hate coyotes."

"Liz said they're harmless."

"I *know* they won't harm us, but hearing the howling sets off some primal fear."

I pried her grip loose from the blanket and intertwined my fingers with hers. She slid her bedroll closer, and we were face-to-face, only inches apart. Her breath smelled of coffee, chocolate, and peanuts.

"I'm sorry. I can't help it."

A third coyote added his voice to the chorus and her grip tightened on my hand.

"They'll quit in a little while," Liz whispered.

In the distance we heard a high-pitched squeal that raised the hairs on the back of my neck. I thought Jill was going to crush my hand.

"They caught a rabbit," Jamie said. "They'll be quiet now."

Jill stared into my eyes, obviously not relieved to know about the dying rabbit nor appreciating the silence of the coyotes. "Only twenty miles from here I have a nice comfortable bed in an apartment where I can't hear the coyotes. There's a coffee maker on a timer, granola for breakfast, and orange juice," she whispered.

"It's more like thirty miles, Jill. We'll have biscuits for breakfast, and I might be able to find some powder to make orange juice," Liz said. "The sun will be up in about seven hours. Some of us need to get a bit of sleep."

"If you took your boots off," Jamie said, "be sure to shake them before you put them on in the morning. The scorpions like to hide in them when the sun rises."

"I thought we weren't telling any ghost stories," Jill whispered.

"That's not a ghost story. I'm just warning you."

"I left my boots on," Jill whispered.

"Me too."

"Jeez, will you guys put a lid on it?" Liz said. "I feel like I'm with the Girl Scouts."

Jill gave my hand a final squeeze, then pulled her hand under her blanket. Her eyes closed and I rolled onto my back so I could stare at the stars. I listened to Jill's breathing, but never heard the slow, easy breaths of a person asleep. I listened to Jamie's raspy respiration, almost a snore, for a few minutes, then I nodded off.

Chapter 17

The shaman sat at the table beneath a blazing gas lantern, his hands wrapped around a plastic glass of scotch. His henchman pushed back the tent flap.

"Are our charges finally asleep, Greg?"

Greg took a seat and poured liquor into an aluminum cup. "I hate this babysitting crap. The new girl is still crying about missing her sisters."

"We need to get Snowflake's mind elsewhere. How much peyote do we have left?"

"We're down to a few buttons. I should call Jerry and get restocked."

"He charges too much. Don't you know someone who can get them cheaper?"

Greg tensed. "Listen, Shamu . . ."

The shaman slammed down his glass. "I'm a shaman, not a damned killer whale. I expect you to address me with respect."

The men glared at each other until Greg looked away.

"Shaman. Shamu. Whatever. You're relying on me for my peyote contacts. When you have your own supplier, you can negotiate the price. As long as we're using *my* guy, we'll pay what he's charging."

The shaman turned red. "I run this camp and I call the shots. When you call Jerry, tell him I want a price break."

"You don't run shit. I'm the one who takes all the risks. I go into the fucking religious compounds and kidnap the kids. The last place was a goddamned concentration camp. They had fences with guards patrolling the compound and people doing headcounts twice a night. I snuck in and grabbed the girl. I took all the risk! All you did was drive the fucking van."

"You can leave any time you want." The shaman glared at Greg. "There aren't many legitimate jobs an ex-convict can get paying what you make."

"Looks like I went from one prison to another. At least El Reno had hot meals and running water. This wilderness camping is bullshit."

"Leave whenever you want."

"You've never paid me, and the only way out is in your van or walking. I went from prison to being a fucking slave."

"Keep your voice down," the shaman hissed. "Once we get these kids back to their parents, you'll get paid. You can go back to Las Vegas and blow it all on call girls and gambling like last time."

"You get your rocks off your way and I get mine my way."

There was a scream from the other tent and they both jumped up. "Damnit! That girl is going to get it one of these times." Greg rushed out with the shaman at his heals.

"Take it easy. The cult had their hooks deep into her psyche. It's going to take a while to undo the programming."

Snowflake sat on the edge of the bed with tears streaming down her face. She glared at them when they pulled back the tent flap. "I want to go home!"

The shaman sat next to her and stroked her hair. "Did you have a vision about your new life?"

"I had a nightmare. I want to go back to my village."

"Your parents are waiting for you."

"I don't want to go back to Yakima!"

"Lay down, Snowflake. We'll show you the way back to controlling your own life. You don't need the village of con men and perverts."

The girl glared at him. "I'm better here with kidnappers who drug me?"

"Shh. Your path will become clear."

Greg, standing next to the tent flap, rolled his eyes. "I'm going back to commune with Johnnie Walker."

Chapter 18

The sky was light when I heard Liz clattering aluminum pans. Jill's bedroll was still spread next to me, but she was out of sight. Jamie added wood to a fire already burnt down to cooking embers.

I pushed myself up on one elbow and stretched. "How long have you guys been up?"

Jamie dropped a branch on the fire, sending sparks flying. "The rest of us have been up for almost an hour. We got tired of trying to be quiet so you could sleep."

I smelled the aroma of instant coffee and got a whiff of biscuits. I heard footsteps behind me. Jill came back from her bathroom trip carrying the shovel and a roll of toilet paper. She nodded to me and gave a slight smile as she passed on her way to the hand sanitizer. There were dark bags under her eyes and her face was ashen, a testimony to her disturbed sleep.

I sat up and my sleeping pad coiled itself. Rather than fighting it, I made a bedroll out of the pad and blanket. My muscles ached from backpacking and sleeping on the ground. My mouth tasted like a mouse had slept in it. I realized Jamie and Liz had already packed away their bedrolls and were moving along with their day.

I sat next to Liz, who pulled the kettle out of the fire. She opened the lid and put steaming biscuits onto the aluminum plates. I poured myself coffee, then accepted a plate from Liz. When Jill finished pouring the brown sugar syrup on her biscuits, she handed the cup to me.

I took a bite of the heavenly steaming biscuit dripping with thin syrup. "Liz, I could marry you."

"I bet you say that to all the girls who cook you breakfast."

I tried to remember the last time a woman had spent the night. It had been in St. Paul, back when I drank heavily. I met a "cop groupie" who'd been hanging around Alary's, a cop hangout. She'd been happy to "hook up" with me, apparently a regular occurrence among the local cops. Very early the next morning I awoke hungover, to the sound of the shower running. It took me a few seconds to piece together the crumpled extra pillow, women's clothes on the floor, and the condom wrapper on the nightstand. When the woman came out of the shower I was struck by her youth, the number and size of tattoos on her body, and the knowing smile on her face. She dressed quickly, declined breakfast, and left without ceremony or any empty promises about calls or emails that would never be sent. Her only words were, "Maybe I'll see you at the bar sometime."

Jill stared at me, apparently reading my thoughts. Then I wondered if she was processing a similar memory in response to Liz's comment.

We finished breakfast in silence, each of us with our own thoughts about the day. Liz and Jamie cleaned and sanitized the dishes while I helped Jill spread the embers of the fire and cover them with dry soil.

"Is this enough to keep the fire from rekindling?"

"Should be. We separated all the embers and they'll die quickly under the dirt."

Jamie and Liz were packed up by the time we were through with the embers. Jill pushed a stick into the ground in the center of the fire ring. I'd seen Jamie do that the previous morning and I thought it odd. "Why did you put the stick there?"

"If there's a forest fire, the investigators can come back here and look for our campsite. If they find the stick still unburned, they know the fire wasn't caused by us."

"Huh," was all I could say.

Jill pulled the scrunchy out of her ponytail and ran her fingers through her hair. She gathered it up and pulled the ponytail together before putting her floppy-brimmed hat back on. She realized I'd been watching her.

"It's definitely a bad hair day. Are we ready to go?"

Liz already had her backpack strapped on and Jamie hoisted his, carefully avoiding the bandage on his shoulder.

I was concerned about his shoulder getting infected. "We should've checked your bandage and put more antiseptic on the wound."

"Liz did that before you got up. It's not inflamed or hot. It looks good."

Liz nodded her assent.

I sat on the flat rock next to my backpack and reached down for the straps. The jolt of pain hit me like grabbing an electrified fence. "Yeow!" I jumped up and started shaking my hand.

Jill rushed over and grabbed my hand. "What happened?"

"I was reaching for my backpack when I got jolted. The pain was a hundred times more painful than the worst bee sting I've ever had."

Liz set her pack down. "I didn't hear a rattlesnake."

Jamie grabbed the top flap and tipped my backpack over. He got on his hands and knees and looked warily under the rock next to the pack. "It looks like a striped-tail scorpion."

Jill looked at my right hand. "Yeah, it's not a snakebite. There's only one little red dot."

"Jeez that hurts. Do we need to call for an evacuation? Can we get a helicopter out?"

Jamie smiled. "Scorpion stings hurt like hell, but they're not fatal. Especially the striped-tail ones. They're pretty innocuous."

Liz took a bottle of Tylenol out of her backpack and shook out two pills. She handed them to me with a water bottle. "These'll help the with the pain, but it's going to hurt for a while."

"Define a while."

Jamie shrugged. "Depends on how much venom you got."

"How big was the scorpion?"

"Not big." Jamie held his fingers about two inches apart. "But they don't always inject all their venom. If you just startled him, he might've just given you a warning jolt. If he felt threatened, he might've given you a full shot."

I shook my hand, willing it to stop throbbing. "Why don't you crawl under the rock and ask him if he was startled or threatened?"

Jill glared at me. "There's no need for sarcasm. You'll be fine and the pain will subside with time."

Liz poured water on a clean bandana and handed it to me. "Hold that on your hand for a couple minutes. A cold compress would be better, but I'm fresh out of ice."

I pressed the bandana against the edge of my hand, below my little finger, then realized the others were all staring. "You're sure I'm not going to die from this?"

Liz shook her head. "There have been two scorpion fatalities in Arizona in the past twenty years, and both of them were children who were stung by bark scorpions. You're going to be fine."

I took the compress off to look at the site of the sting and I wiggled my fingers. "The pain is a little better, but my whole hand is starting to swell and my fingers tingle."

Jamie looked at my hand, then glanced at my holster. "I hope we don't meet any bad guys for a while. That's your shooting hand."

Liz smiled. "Now that I've proven my shooting skills, maybe I should carry the gun."

I shook my hand and flexed my fingers. "That's not happening. Let's go."

Jill lifted my backpack and helped me with the straps. Once again, I caught the waist strap on the butt of my pistol but adjusted it so I had access to the Sig. Jill watched, looking like she could fall asleep standing up. I helped her get the backpack adjusted on her shoulders.

"It helps that we're drinking up my load," Jill said. "I'm down twenty pounds of water."

Jamie and Liz were already trekking down the trail when Jill cinched the last of her backpack straps. We set off at a comfortable pace. I knew we'd consumed quite a bit of the water from my backpack, but it didn't feel much lighter, probably due to my muscles aching after another day of hiking.

I fell in step alongside Jill. "Did you get any sleep after the coyotes stopped howling?"

"Not much."

"What's with you and the coyotes?"

"I had a bad camping experience."

"You just about gave me a heart attack when you grabbed my shirt in the dark."

"Sorry. It's reflex."

"It seemed like a bit of an overreaction."

We walked for a few minutes without speaking.

"I led a Girl Scout group in Big Bend National Park. We'd set up camp for the evening and were finishing supper. I'd seen a coyote hanging around, and I'd attributed his brazenness to previous groups who'd fed him. He wasn't being aggressive, but he didn't leave, either. We were finishing supper when he came into camp and started edging closer to us. He looked mangy and his tail was hairless. I surmised he was a sick outcast.

"One of the girls was talking to her friend and when she saw the coyote. She screamed and dropped her plate. That started some hysteria. I tried to quiet the girls down, but they all gathered around me.

"I yelled at him and waved my arms, but the coyote had been around people too much and his hunger overcame his natural fear. He raced up to the closest plate and started wolfing down the spilled food. I pushed the girls back and grabbed a piece of wood. When I approached him, he bared his teeth and snarled at me. I decided to back away and took a defensive stance in front of the girls while he worked his way from plate to plate, eating the spilled food. When he'd wolfed down everything, he stared at me for a couple seconds before skulking off.

"Something in his eyes made my skin crawl. It was primal, like he was a predator and I was prey. It scared me right to my roots. I reported the incident when we got back to the trailhead, and a government trapper was dispatched. He caught the coyote within a day and killed it. He showed me the carcass in his pickup and he asked if it was the mangy critter that had scared us. I felt stupid, like I should've been able to chase the thing off, but I just said I thought it was the same animal. He told me it was sick and, although the Park Service wasn't going to pay to have it tested because no one had been bitten, he thought it might've been rabid."

"That's more than a little scary."

Jill shivered. "It's just . . ." She walked a little closer, until our arms were nearly touching. "I'm happy to have you along. You reached for the pistol when I grabbed you."

"Sorry. It was a reflex."

"Don't be sorry. It made me feel . . . secure." We took a few more steps and she looked at me. "I hope you didn't mind holding my hand. I felt a little like a scared kid."

I reached out and squeezed her hand. "It's okay."

"Your thoughts drifted when Liz made the comment about women cooking you breakfast. You zoned out for a while and you weren't smiling. That must not have been a pleasant memory."

I scrambled for a politically correct answer. "I don't have a lot of pleasant memories of my ex-wife."

Jill gave me a knowing grin. "You weren't thinking about your ex-wife." She didn't press the issue, and I didn't offer more.

"How's your hand?"

I tried to flex my fingers but they felt like overstuffed sausages. "It's better, but it's swelling."

"Ideally, it should've been iced and elevated. Walking with it hanging down is aggravating the swelling. We could rig up a sling."

I used my left hand to unbutton one eyelet on my shirt and rested my right wrist in the opening.

Jill helped me refasten the button. "Is that better?"

"It helps the aching. I hope I don't trip or I'll do a face plant on the trail."

We followed the arroyo around a bend. Jamie and Liz were out of their packs and standing by a domed sweat lodge next to an area washed out by the flood. It was covered with a blue plastic tarp. I thought the blue looked inappropriate in the brown, sage green, and tan environment we'd been walking for two days. Then I noticed Jamie squatting next to something on the ground.

"There's been a fire here recently." He poked at the ground with a stick, then he put his palm flat on the ground. "It's still warm. This is from last night. Whoever made this just left it to burn out. They didn't bury the embers."

Jill glanced around. "They might be close."

Jamie stood up and shook his head. "I scouted the area and there's no one close. Just a trail leading down this smaller arroyo.

I slipped off my backpack, carefully keeping it away from anything that could hide a scorpion or snake. "Maybe they stayed around until it burned out."

"Maybe they're just idiots and they walked away from the site without dealing with the fire. They're not Native or from the Park Service." He stood up and walked around the dome, searching the ground.

"There's a well-used trail over here. We'll explore it in a bit." Jamie sniffed the air.

Jill tilted her head back and sniffed, too. "What do you smell, Jamie?"

Liz froze. "Something dead?"

"Why don't you guys stay here with Doug, in case the campfire builders return. I'm going up the ravine."

Liz fell into step with Jamie. "Jill can stay with Doug. I'm going with you."

* * *

I sat on my backpack, making sure I could reach the Sig with my left hand if someone came down the trail. Jill knelt next to me and pulled my hand out of my shirt.

"I think the swelling is going down. How does it feel?"

I flexed my swollen fingers. "It aches. Mostly it feels like my fingers are fat and stiff. I don't think I could pull the trigger with my right hand."

Jill glanced at the trail. "What if someone shows up?"

"I've been taught to shoot with both hands. Help me move the holster to my other hip."

Jill loosened my belt and pulled the holster free, then attached it on the left side. "The butt's pointing the wrong way. Can you draw it and fire?"

I put my left hand on the butt. "I'm not going to win any quick draw competition, but I'll be able to get the pistol out and fire it."

Jamie appeared with Liz a few steps behind. He was as expressionless as a poker player, but Liz looked distraught.

Jamie took out a water bottle and drank from it. "We found a spot where it looks like a shallow grave was eroded open. The soil smells like carrion."

I nodded. "Were you able to collect any evidence?"

"It all washed away with the body or got carried away by vermin. If not for the smell, I don't know I'd have identified that spot as a grave."

I thought to myself, *If Jamie couldn't have identified that spot, no one without a carrion sniffing dog would ever have known it was there.*

"C'mon, Doug, let's check out the trail."

Liz put up here hand. "You *boys* aren't leaving us behind while you check out the trail. The last time you left me behind didn't go well. We're coming along."

Jamie realized he'd already lost the argument. "Okay. Everyone take a drink and leave your packs here. We're going to follow the trail."

Jill interrupted the discussion. "Liz, get the sat phone. Jamie, hang on for a minute."

It took almost five minutes for the phone to power up and connect with the satellites. Jill dialed a number. She didn't try to separate from us. The conversation she planned wasn't meant to be private.

"Brad, it's Jill. Do you have any news from the medical examiner?" She listened, nodding occasionally. "So, he couldn't determine the cause of death because of the decomposition, but the tox screen showed peyote in her tissues. Got it. And they contacted her parents after the I.D."

Jill clenched her jaw as she listened. "Hang on."

She handed the phone to me. "This is Doug. Jill just handed me the phone. I'm not sure why."

"The medical examiner got a preliminary identification on Jane Doe. She'd been reported missing a month ago by her minister. The local police contacted her parents and they told them she wasn't missing, they had her 'removed' from a cult and she was being reprogrammed. Her parents hadn't been contacted by the reprogramming group, so they didn't know she was dead. The M.E. verified the identification through dental records. The parents didn't know how to contact the reprogramming people except through their website."

"Where's this reprogramming group located?"

"The M.E. accessed their website, but there isn't a physical address listed. The only contact method offered is a cellphone number with a Utah area code and it wasn't answered. He left a message but hasn't had a return call."

"The M.E. said she was Native. Do her parents live on the reservation?"

"Her mother is Navajo. Her father is white. They live near Sedona."

"We found a sweat lodge on the Rez, across the river from the Park Service land. Did your search for fake sweat operators get any hits?"

"There are a couple groups out of Sedona who do sweats. They've been there a few years and they seem to run safe operations. After talking to the M.E. I looked specifically for anyone doing cult reprogramming and I found the website the parents told the M.E. about. It says they use traditional methods, but like the M.E. said, there's no way to contact them except by leaving a message. I called and left my cellphone number, but they haven't returned my call."

"That's great information." I paused, thinking about Jill's anger during her conversation with Brad. I turned away from the others and took a couple steps. "Why was Jill so distracted when you spoke to her?"

"Um, I don't think I can comment."

"If there's something that's going to affect her judgment, I need to know about it. We may be close to the reprogramming people."

"One of the volunteers overheard a Park Service bigshot talking on the phone. Jill's going to be suspended while the Park Service investigates the flash flood deaths. The ranger grapevine says her suspension might not be resolved until the lawsuit brought by the family is settled, which might take years. Please don't say anything to her. At this point it's all rumors."

I took a deep breath and glanced at Jill, who stared absently down the ravine while Jamie and Liz talked. "Thanks, Brad." I told him our location.

"What are you going to do?"

"We're going to follow the backtrail from the sweat lodge we found. Please advise the Navajo Nation Police we're investigating the possible death of a girl on the Rez. Call us if you don't hear from us in an hour. If we don't answer, send backup."

"Do you want the sheriff's department or the Navajo Police?"

"I have no idea what we're walking into. Call them both."

I disconnected and handed the phone to Jamie. "I think you'd better call your office. We may need some backup."

Jamie handed the phone to Liz. "I don't want to call unless we've got trouble."

Jill explained Jamie's reaction. "Jamie is accustomed to working alone. Doug, as a former big city cop, is used to having backup."

Jamie nodded toward the holster on my left hip. "Your right hand isn't functional?"

I held up my swollen fingers. "I'm not sure my fingers will fit inside the trigger guard."

Jamie nodded. "Even lefthanded you're a hundred percent more backup than I'm used to."

I nodded. "We're all going. Liz, keep the sat phone powered up and have the tribal police on speed dial in case we need to call in the cavalry."

Jamie looked as annoyed as I'd ever seen him. "Calling the cavalry isn't a phrase you want to use on the Rez. Cavalry attacks don't evoke the same sense of rescue for Natives as they do for whites."

I put up my hand. "I apologize. Liz will call for backup."

"Liz, give the phone back to Jill." Jamie dug in his backpack, pulled out a tattered red bandana, untied it, and unwrapped a small pistol. He pulled back the slide, checked to make sure it was loaded, then released the slide. It slid shut with a click.

"This is a Glock 42," Jamie explained, handing the small gun to Liz butt-first. "There's no safety to release. You just pull the trigger and it'll fire until the magazine is empty."

Liz turned the gun in her hand, studying it, but keeping it safely pointed away from the rest of us. "I shot my dad's Glock, but this one's tiny. I've shot .22 pistols bigger than this."

"It's a .380, which is more powerful than a .22, but it's not going to stop a charging bull. There are only six shots, but I know you can make them count if you need to."

Liz smiled at the compliment and slipped the small pistol into her right pocket. "Is this your backup gun?"

"It's more like my gun of last resort. I have it, but if I have to rely on that peashooter, I'm in deep trouble."

Jill's conversation with Brad had left her antsy. "Let's go."

Jamie led us down the trail that went straight when the arroyo veered right and snaked downward. We stopped when we came to a crest in the hill above a grove of pine trees.

Jamie signaled for us to stop and whispered. "This grove would be a logical place for someone to set up camp."

Chapter 19

There wasn't any cover to conceal our approach, but the dry ground and whistling wind hid the sound of our footsteps. Jamie put up his hand when we got to the first tree. The pine grove appeared forest-like from afar. Now that we'd reached the edge, I could see trees spaced apart, more park-like than I'd anticipated and affording no cover for our approach. The murmur of voices was audible, and I saw parts of two large tents near the other edge of the pines thirty yards away.

Jamie leaned close. "It'd probably be good if you pinned on your badge. Having two law enforcement people here might keep a lid on things better than just me showing up with three civilians.

I took out my wallet and unpinned the Park Service badge from the leather. In a fumbled attempt to pin it to my shirt with my swollen hand, I managed to stick myself in the chest. Jill took the badge from me and pinned it neatly over my left pocket and patted the badge once, like she was wishing me good luck.

Jamie waited until Jill was done. "I'm going to walk in like I own the place. You guys hang back behind some cover."

I nodded my understanding and upped my respect for Jamie. It took guts to walk alone into an unknown situation.

Liz grabbed Jamie's arm. "How will we know if you need help? Do you have a codeword we should react to?"

"If I yell Doug's name, come running." He patted her hand. "Keep the Glock in your pocket. It may be our ace in the hole."

Liz rubbed her pocket, fingering the outline of the gun. "Okay."

Jamie marched up the trail and we moved to a spot where some bushes partially hid us. We could now see the two large white canvas tents and hear men's voices. Two vehicles were parked on the edge of the trees: A white Ford van looked like it could seat a dozen people. The other was a battered pickup. Both were covered in dust.

The voices stopped when Jamie pulled back the tent flap. "What's going on?"

The response to his question wasn't audible, but the tone of the voices sounded angry.

"You're on the Navajo Reservation. You've got no business here."

There were muted angry words in response.

Jamie pushed back the tent flap with his forearm and looked for us. I stood up and he nodded. "Doug."

With his hand out of sight from the people inside the tent he gestured for Liz and Jill to stay hidden.

I stepped out from behind the bushes. "I don't like the look of this, Jill. Call the cavalry."

She punched numbers into the phone. "Stall. No one's going to get here quickly."

The tent was lit only by the sunlight filtering through the white canvas. Two men sat at a folding table and a third stood beside them. I thought the standing man was trying to look like Jesus. His long white robe was belted with a rope and he clasped his hands in front of his waist. His salt-and-pepper hair flowed over his shoulders. His beard and moustache were nearly white and went to the middle of his chest. I perceived no threat from him, but I'd been fooled by appearances so kept him in my peripheral vision.

One of the seated men wore a coarse cotton pullover shirt. The other man was in western garb including a sweat-stained Stetson. Both had their hands on the table near cellphones. Between them was a stack of money. A pile of green knobs, that I assumed were peyote buttons, had spilled from a purple cloth bag. I wondered if there was cellphone coverage here, then it occurred to me some phones could also be used as walkie-talkies to communicate with each other even if they couldn't reach a cell tower. The table hid their waists so I couldn't tell if they were armed or not. Behind the men were folding chairs arranged in two rows.

The standing man appraised me and studied my badge. "Park Service? We're not in a park." He spoke in a deep baritone voice.

"I'm a Federal law enforcement officer. I have jurisdiction anywhere in the United States." That was a little bit of a stretch, but the oath I took said I was to uphold the laws of the United States and protect against foes, foreign and domestic. There was nothing in the oath about enforcement only on Park Service land. The orders to keep my firearm nearby 24/7 reinforced my belief I had far ranging powers . . . and enforcement responsibilities.

The standing man's eyes narrowed as he considered my comment. "As I told your Native friend, we're on private land and we're operating with the permission of the landowner." The other men nodded.

Jamie's thumbs were resting on his belt, and I assumed he'd be able to draw his pistol faster than the seated men could react. I thought about the Sig on my left hip, and realized I'd demonstrated proficiency shooting lefthanded, but I'd never pulled my weapon from the holster with my left hand.

"Your map reading skills need some work." Jamie nodded toward the green nobs on the table. "And those look like peyote buttons."

The Jesus figure smiled, but his voice was sharp. "I don't see how that's any of your concern."

"Peyote is illegal and possessing it is a crime."

"The Supreme Court ruled peyote can be used in Native religious ceremonies. I'm an Indian shaman."

Jamie smiled. "Really? Which tribe?"

"I trained with the Shoshone in Nebraska."

"Do you remember crossing a deep arroyo on your way here, the one lined with trees on both sides?"

None of the men showed any reaction to Jamie's words.

"That's the Little Colorado River, the border of the Navajo Reservation. I'm not sure what standing a Shoshone shaman, who looks white, will have in a Navajo court."

The two men at the table looked at the standing man, who appeared to be considering Jamie's words.

Jamie held out his hand and stepped toward the table. "Show me your identification."

The standing man lifted his hand to his face like he was going to stroke his beard. Alarms sounded in my brain telling me he was signaling the others or diverting my attention. I looked away from him at the two seated men, and reached for the Sig. The cowboy was sliding his hand away from the pile of peyote buttons when I drew my pistol with my left hand and fumbled with the safety with my swollen right hand. The expression on the faces of the three men said I looked like an amateur.

I kept the Sig pointed at the floor with my finger alongside the trigger guard. "Keep your hands on the table. Tell my partner where your I.D. is and he'll take it out."

The standing man seemed to speak for everyone. "I carry no worldly items. I am Shaman Saampunku."

Jamie walked behind the table and searched the men's pockets. The cowboy had a large wallet with a chain running to his belt and a Colt .45 single-action revolver in a quick draw holster. Jamie unloaded the Colt, letting the cartridges fall on the table. The other man's pockets were empty.

Jamie opened the wallet and took out a driver's license. "Jerry Melton. Are you the seller?"

The man stared at Jamie with hatred in his eyes. "The chief can use them legally. I just collect them. I've been paid, so I can leave you Indians to sort out who has jurisdiction."

I took a step closer to the table. "No, you're going to sit there while we sort this out." I looked more closely at the chairs behind the men and realized each of them had handcuffs chained to the legs. "Why do you need handcuffs on the chairs?"

The shaman glanced over his shoulder. "We reprogram people after they get out of religious sects. Sometimes they need to be restrained to protect them from themselves."

I nodded toward the green buttons. "Is the peyote part of the retraining?"

"It helps people gain clarity." The shaman put up his hands. "Listen, we're running a legitimate and legal operation. People turn their loved ones over to me when they've got nowhere else to turn."

Jamie moved to the folding chairs and looked at the handcuffs. "You use peyote and sweats to get them to change. I take it some of them don't entirely buy into the reprogramming. There's blood on this set of handcuffs."

The shaman's eyes never left me. "It's not a pretty process. They've bought into the cults and given their money, and sometimes their bodies, to the leaders. Think about Jim Jones in Guyana. He had those people so programmed they were willing to give their children cyanide laced drinks."

Jamie sat in one of the chairs. "Let's get back to the peyote." Shaman Saampunku had turned to look at Jamie, which gave me a look at the back of his robe. There were pockets on each side and the right pocket bulged. Whatever was in the pocket looked heavy.

Jamie nodded. "To legally use it, you have to be conducting a Native religious ceremony."

The shaman struggled to maintain his composure. "I'm familiar with the statute."

I watched him carefully, keeping the Sig against my leg. I moved slightly to my right so Jamie wasn't in the line of fire if I had to shoot the shaman. The other two men were ignoring the exchange between the shaman and Jamie. They watched me with their hands on the table. The amount of money was considerable—a stack of twenties, fifties, and hundred-dollar bills had tipped over when Jamie interrupted the transaction. The peyote buttons had spilled onto the table from a purple cloth bag. I could see dozens of them, and the bag was swollen with more.

Jamie smiled. "Shaman is more of an East Indian term. We usually refer to the people who conduct sweat ceremonies as elders. Perhaps the shaman title is more common with the Shoshone people you trained with in Nebraska."

Jamie's words struck something with the shaman. His confidence slipped slightly.

"I chose the title shaman because it's meaningful to the people who bring their loved ones to me for reprogramming. The Shoshones used the term 'fathers' when referring to their spiritual leaders."

The shaman lost some of his arrogance and he seemed a bit nervous. The two men at the table maintained their rigid posture and appeared ready to spring into action. The situation seemed off, but Jamie didn't seem to be catching the vibe. He focused on the shaman.

"I'm very surprised you were trained in Nebraska."

"There are large reservations there and the people were welcoming. They have drug and alcohol problems, as well

241

as some cult issues. They were constantly training new leaders who were using sweat ceremonies to help turn their people to a better pathway."

I heard a moan from outside the tent. Soft voices followed.

Jamie looked over his shoulder at the tent wall behind him. "It sounds like someone is waking up. What's in your other tent?"

"Our clients sleep and eat there. They come here for discussion and training."

"How many clients are you currently reprogramming?"

"Five."

I guessed if they were reprogramming five people, the shaman and the man dressed in white weren't the only staff. I moved farther from the tent flap so I could watch the opening, rather than standing with my back to it. That move seemed to worry the two men at the table. The situation felt wrong and my swollen right hand throbbed. I adjusted my grip on the Sig, which caught the attention of the two seated men.

Jamie continued to be oblivious to the changing dynamics of the three men. He couldn't see their faces. They looked too smug given the situation.

"I find it interesting you chose to train with the Nebraska Shoshone people. The Nebraska Omaha and Paiute tribes don't like other tribes very well and I'm surprised they'd let a Shoshone from Nevada or Utah train a white medicine man on their reservations."

I was amazed at how chatty Jamie had become, and realized he'd led the shaman into a verbal trap.

The shaman's icy confidence was melting. "I trained in Nevada, too."

"Is that where they gave the Shoshone name Saampunku to you?"

"Saampunku is the name bestowed upon me in a solemn ceremony after I'd completed my training."

Jamie's smile told me he'd nailed the shaman. "Saampunku is the Shoshone name for devil. You may have been called that, but I seriously doubt anyone bestowed that name on you."

Just outside the tent flap I heard Jill. "Get your hands off me!" I raised the Sig as the tent flap opened. Jill and Liz were pushed into the tent by a large, bearded man who had a pistol pointed at Liz.

Folding chairs clattered and out of the corner of my eye I saw the chairs tumbling as the bottom of the tent wall moved. Jamie was gone, apparently having rolled off the chairs and under the back wall of the tent. That left me trying to cover four men spread around the large area of the tent, one of them pointing an old single-action six shooter at Liz's back while holding one of Jill's arms. Liz stood ahead of Jill with her hands in the air.

The gunman looked confident. "Look who I found hiding in the bushes."

The shaman turned to me. "Lower your gun."

Jerry, the cowboy, grabbed his pistol from the tabletop and I turned my gun toward him. "Don't." His gun was still unloaded, but he eyed the cartridges Jamie had dumped on the table.

The shaman raised his hands in front of him. "Let's all take it easy. No one has been hurt. This is just a misunderstanding." He looked at Jill and Liz, noting their Park Service uniforms and badges. "More rangers outside the park."

The shaman nodded toward the gunman. "Greg, move the women away from the entry. The Indian just went out of the back and he has a gun too."

The cowboy stood up while keeping his hand near the pistol. "Listen, shaman. I came here to deliver some product. I didn't sign on for killing park rangers."

The shaman took another step toward me. "No one's been killed. If Mr. Ranger sets down his gun, I think we can let everyone leave quietly. They've got a long walk back to civilization. By the time they get there we'll be in Nevada or Utah."

The shaman put out his hand and took two more steps toward me, to take my gun. I pointed it at his stomach and dropped my finger from the trigger guard to the trigger. The significance of the move wasn't lost on him. He stopped and raised his hands.

"It appears your dominant hand is injured. I don't think you'd do very well with your left if Glen got an itchy trigger finger."

I smiled and stalled, hoping Jamie had a plan. "We're trained to shoot with either hand. I group my shots in the ten-ring with my right hand. I can only stay inside the nine-ring with my left."

There were whispers outside the tent and the sound of someone retching. The shaman and gunman were nervous and I knew the situation could degenerate quickly.

"Greg has a gun pointed at your colleagues. I suggest you not do anything stupid. Everyone can walk away from this."

Jill jerked her arm away from the gunman and rubbed her wrist. "What about the people you're 'treating'? Can they leave with us?"

The shaman shook his head. "Their families pay us handsomely to reprogram them. They'll come with us."

"There are five kids handcuffed to cots over here," Jamie yelled from outside the tent. "I think one of the guys is on a bad peyote trip. He's aspirating on vomit."

Liz lowered her hands. "I'm an EMT. Let me help."

The shaman did a quick assessment of Liz, then nodded. She turned and ran out of the tent.

The gunman shifted his aim to Jill's back. "I don't think we should've given up a hostage."

The shaman glared at the gunman. "And I don't think we can afford to let one of our clients die."

I put up my right hand. "I'll tell you what should happen. Greg puts his gun on the ground, I take my finger off the trigger, and we all take a deep breath."

The shaman nodded to the gunman, but Greg continued to point the gun at Jill's spine. "This isn't going to play out like that. My gun doesn't go on the ground. The shaman and his flunkies may be willing to play along with you, but I'm not going back to prison."

He swung his gun away from Jill and pointed it at the shaman. "Toss me the van keys and I'll go away. The rest of you can play with the Park Service however you want."

The shaman put out his hands. "Nothing's happened, Greg. We can sort this all out and walk away."

The gunman shook his head. "They're here because of the dead girl."

The shaman's eyes shot from Greg to me. I kept my best poker face and let him guess what we might or might not know.

The shaman watched me carefully and he put his right hand in his pocket. "I'm reaching into my pocket for the keys,"

I nodded. "Slowly."

The shaman lowered his right hand, reached into his pocket, and came out with a keyring. He tossed it to Greg.

The gunman dropped the keys into his pocket and pushed Jill toward the table. "As long as I'm leaving, I'd might as well take the pile of cash with me. Stuff the money into the bag."

Jill dumped the peyote buttons on the table and stuffed the money into the bag. She took a step toward the gunman, then handed the bag to him.

Liz appeared at the tent flap looking rattled, her uniform splattered with vomit. "We need to get the kid out of here. He needs medical attention or he's going to die."

The gunman stepped away from the tent flap. "You guys can do whatever you want. But not until I'm gone. The girl's going with me." He pulled Jill to the flap, then let go of her and grabbed Liz's collar. "You're my driver." He pulled her out the tent, the flap closing behind them.

Jill's look of terror at the prospect of Liz being a hostage propelled me into motion. "Shaman, what've you got in your pocket?"

He reached down and pulled out a stun gun. "I have to use it occasionally to subdue a client who's out of control."

I took it from him and handed it to Jill. "Here. Keep these guys under control."

I stopped at the tent flap and peeked around to make sure I wouldn't get ambushed. Greg pushed Liz into the passenger's seat of the van. I looked around for Jamie, but he'd vanished. With Liz inside the van, Greg pushed her over the hump toward the driver's seat. I ran toward the van as she fell headfirst into the driver's door. Greg batted at her feet, trying to get her over a console and into the driver's seat while she kicked at him.

Greg's pistol fired and the driver's window exploded over Liz's head. Greg's shot was followed by six rapid shots. Greg looked stunned but was still upright.

I raised my Sig, but was afraid to fire, especially left-handed, while Greg was so close to Liz. The driver's door flew open and Liz tumbled out with the little Glock in her hand. Two more shots rang out, punching holes in the windshield and splattering it with blood. I ducked and dashed right to get out of the line of fire as Liz ran toward me. She threw her arms around my neck and Greg crumpled inside the van. The whole gunfight had taken less than ten seconds, even though it seemed to play out in slow motion.

Liz sobbed. "Is he dead?"

I patted her back. "He's out of action and you're safe. Are there any more of the shaman's men in the other tent?"

"No."

"Are you injured?"

"I don't think so."

I held her back and picked a few pieces of glass from her hair. I checked her scalp and upper body for blood but

248

found no wounds. I carefully took the Glock from her shaking hand and slipped it into my waistband, then hugged her while she shook.

I tried to keep my voice from quivering now the adrenaline was leaving my system. "You did well. It's over now."

Jamie climbed out of the van through the side door and walked to the passenger's door where Greg's body was slumped against the dashboard. He took the pistol from Greg's hand and dropped it into his pocket.

"Do we need an ambulance, Jamie?"

Jamie shook his head. "Not for him. Is Liz okay?"

I nodded, peeled Liz free, and pushed her toward Jamie. She latched onto him and sobbed. I jogged back to the tent where Jill held the stun gun straight out in front of her, as if it was a real gun.

When she saw me, Jill lowered her hand. "What was the shooting?"

"Liz escaped and shot Greg."

Jill handed me the stun gun. "Is Liz all right?"

"Physically, yes."

Jill ran past me to check on Liz, leaving me with the three men. "Put your hands behind your heads, face away from me, and interlace your fingers." I took out my keyring and unlocked handcuffs from the chairs, then clipped them onto the men's wrists.

Chapter 20

Jill and I were sitting on vinyl covered chairs in the Navajo National Police station hallway. She squirmed in her seat. "Do you think these chairs were this uncomfortable fifty years ago when they were new?"

"You've been sleeping on the ground for two nights and you're complaining about the chairs?" That comment got me a glare. "At least I'm close to an electrical outlet so I can charge my dead cellphone."

"What were you told on the drive here?" Jill had ridden in the Coconino County SUV that had arrived moments ahead of the Navajo Nation Police.

"Jamie's boss, Ray Horn, confirmed the guy who'd shot at us in the hills was indeed suffering from plague. He'd contracted it from the flea bites covering his body or exposure to the blood from the rodents they'd been handled and eaten. He's in the hospital receiving IV antibiotics. The doctor suggested all of us who'd been exposed to him be treated with Cipro."

Jill squirmed in her chair again. "How long has Jamie been in with Ray Horn?"

I looked at the clock on my cellphone. "He's been in Captain Horn's office with the door closed for nearly half an

251

hour. Liz is being interviewed by a female officer. No one seems to care what we have to say."

"Yeah, they seem to have forgotten us."

I looked around. The desk across from us was unattended and I couldn't even hear voices. "I'm dying for a cup of brewed coffee. I wonder if there's a break room with a coffee pot somewhere nearby."

"Tell me what happened while I held the shaman at bay with the stun gun."

"Greg shoved Liz in the van kicking and screaming and the kidnapper's gun went off. Luckily the shot went over her head. She pulled Jamie's Glock and fired all six shots, then rolled out the door. Jamie expected the van to be used as the escape vehicle, so he hid in the back. When the firing started in the front seat he'd jumped up and saw Liz's shots hit the gunman. Greg raised his pistol for another shot at Liz when Jamie fired from the rear of the van. His shots killed the gunman."

"You never fired a shot?"

"I never got the chance. Where did you go while I handcuffed the shaman?"

"We found five people shackled to cots. One was covered in his own vomit and another was hallucinating. The others were awake, but afraid of everyone but Liz. They were all taken to the hospital where they'll be able to contact their families."

"I wonder if they'll suffer flashbacks from the peyote and the repeated sweat ceremonies?"

Jill closed her eyes and shook her head. "They'll probably be messed up for the rest of their lives."

"Ray Horn interviewed one the reprogramming subjects. They confirmed that polygamy was part of the sect she'd been in. She told them the minister and male elders had "initiated" girls as young as twelve, taking them as wives. They welcomed their pregnancies as gifts from God. Because their business office was off the reservation, the U.S. Marshals were interviewing the rest of the survivors and making plans to coordinate raids of the religious compounds with local sheriffs' offices."

"I overheard one of the marshals say they were getting search warrants for the Utah sect's compound. They were strategizing ways to avoid another Waco siege and the loss of life."

My smartphone chirped, telling me it was fully charged. "I wonder if any of this has made the news yet?" I flipped through icons on my home pages until I found the BBC and AP icons. "There's nothing on the wire services."

"Doug, this story needs to get out. We should put our own spin on it before the news media hear about it from the shaman and his lawyer."

I paged through my call history until I found Sarah Hawkins's number at *The Santa Fe Journal*. She'd written a series of articles about the drug and antiquities smuggling ring Jamie and I had stumbled across during a murder investigation. She'd been a bulldog of a reporter and had managed to publish the articles without mentioning me as her source and before the FBI held a press conference to claim credit for busting the case open. I touched 'return call' and waited for Sarah's voicemail.

Jill frowned. "Who are you calling?"

I put up my finger, intending to leave Sarah a message.

"Doug Fletcher, is that you?"

I tilted the phone so Jill could listen. "Yeah, Sarah. It's me. How are you?"

"You thought you were going to get my machine, didn't you?"

"Busted. How did you know it was me?"

"We have this amazing invention called caller I.D. It tells me who's calling before I pick up. Did you call to congratulate me for winning the New Mexico Press Association award for breaking your story about the antiquities theft ring, or is there something else on your mind?"

"Congratulations. I've been in a training program in Georgia and I missed the news about you winning the journalism prize."

"Thanks. Without your information, I wouldn't have had the story."

"Are you ready for another story?"

"I'm sitting in front of my laptop. What should I type?"

"Hang on, I'm here with Jill Rickowski. I'm going to put you on speakerphone."

"Hi, Jill. You're Doug's boss, right?"

"I'd rather say we're colleagues. But yes, we're working together out of the Flagstaff Park Service office."

"What's up?"

Jill pushed the phone toward me. "The Navajo Nation police just arrested three men in connection with the death of a Navajo girl who's been missing for two weeks. The men have been operating a cult reprogramming camp on the Navajo Reservation and the girl died during one of their sweat lodge ceremonies."

"Where are you getting this information?"

"We were there when they were arrested. A fourth man was killed in a gunfight with a Park Service ranger and a Navajo Nation policeman."

"Were you the ranger in the gunfight, Doug?"

"No. I was away from the action."

"Okay. So, where was this and who was involved?" We could hear Sarah's computer keys clicking in the background.

"On the Navajo reservation, north of Flagstaff."

"There's nothing on the wire services about this."

I pushed the phone back to Jill. "It ties in with a story from last week. The Park Service recovered a woman's body in the Little Colorado River flats bordering Wupatki National Monument and the reservation. It washed out of a shallow grave by the flash flood."

"Hang on. I'm on the Reuters News Service site looking for stories about an Arizona flash flood. It's searching. Okay, I've got a story about hikers in Wupatki who were rescued." She paused. "You lost three hikers but recovered four bodies. Jane Doe has been unidentified, and the cause of her death is under investigation.

"You've got my attention and I understand the context of a Park Service investigator being involved. Fill me in on the details. Spell Rickowski for me."

"You can't attribute this story to me. I'm already in hot water with the Park Service."

"Give me a break. Doug and I played this game of ring-around-the-rosy last time. I don't have time to jump through all the hoops to avoid divulging my sources. What's the story?"

I pulled the phone back. "I'll work a quid pro quo deal with you. I'll give you the story about the reprogramming camp, but you'll have to call the president of the Navajo Nation to make the second part work."

"Why would he talk to me?"

"He doesn't want to talk to you or the person you're going to introduce to him."

"I don't like the sound of this."

"The Surgeon General wants to talk about the Indian Health Services. I need the door to get cracked open on the reservation's end."

"And just how did you divine that the Surgeon General wants to talk to the Navajo Nation President?"

"We spoke on a plane ride."

"Now you're starting to sound scary. I wrote a story about the Surgeon General meeting with the Border Patrol and Homeland Security in Flagstaff. Were you really on the plane with him?"

"I can give you a phone number that will get you directly to the Surgeon General's adjutant. Will that give me credibility?"

"That would certainly be a start." Sarah paused and I heard computer keys clicking. "Tell me about the girl's body found after the flash flood, and the re-programming camp arrests."

I passed the phone to Jill, who took it with resignation. "There were four bodies. Three were campers . . ."

Chapter 21

The drive in the dark from Shiprock to Flagstaff was miserable and I struggled to stay awake. I was surprised to find Jill parked outside my townhouse. She was out of the Park Service pickup before I shut off the engine.

I waved her toward the door. "I've been thinking about what you told the reporter."

She waited for me to unlock and open the door. "You're a hero again."

"I didn't do squat. Jamie and Liz had a shootout with the shaman's guy. All I did was cuff the men in the tent."

I held the door for Jill. "That's a nice story, but Sarah's going to interview Jamie and Liz, and they're going to corroborate the version I told her."

"But . . ." I threw the keys on the counter in exasperation and opened the refrigerator. "I hope you liked the grapefruit-flavored fizzy water. I haven't been to a store yet, and that's all I have left over from my cousin's visit."

"Before I forget it, you have to help fill out the paperwork because Liz discharged your firearm."

I sat on the sofa and popped my can of water. "Crap."

Jill sat next to me on the sofa. My front door swung open, surprising both of us. I reached for the Sig.

Sheila stuck her head in. "Knock, knock. I brought your mail. I hope I'm not interrupting anything."

Jill quickly slid to the far end of the sofa, spilling some soda on the cushion in her rush to create separation. She put on her best professional smile, but I saw red start creeping up from her collar. I got up and met Sheila a step inside the door.

"Thanks. I didn't know you had a key for my box."

"I caught the mailman sorting your mail. I told him I was going to save you a trip to the box." Sheila craned her head around the support column at the end of the breakfast nook, giving Jill a glistening smile. "Hi. I'm Sheila, Doug's neighbor."

Jill gave Sheila her best dazzling smile. "I know. We met at the grocery store last summer."

It took Sheila a second to connect the woman on my couch wearing the Park Service uniform with Jill in shorts and a tank top, standing in front of the steaks in the grocery store. "You're Doug's boss."

"We're colleagues."

Sheila put her hand on my arm. "I've got beer, chips, and pico de gallo. Come over after your company is gone and we can catch up on what's happened since you went away to school."

Jill tapped her watch. "Doug, we're going to be late for our reservation."

"I'm sorry. I'll have to take another rain check."

Sheila leaned close and whispered. "You're dating her?"

I nodded.

Sheila pecked me on the cheek. "You're into cougars. That's cool."

Jill was at my elbow when Sheila closed the door. "I think we'd better get out of your townhouse. The Park Service rumor mill will be buzzing if anyone sees my truck parked here."

I grabbed my keys. "Too late. Sheila thought it was cool I'm dating a cougar. I imagine that story will get around town."

Jill rolled her eyes. "I'm a cougar? C'mon, I'm driving."

We went to Black Bart's Steakhouse. Jill waved off the offer of the wine list and ordered Diet Coke. I had the rib eye. Jill decided to be healthy and chose a Caesar salad with chicken.

When the waiter left, I leaned back in my chair. "Are we going to discuss my future like the last time we were here?"

"I wish you'd stay in Flagstaff."

"I've already rented a townhouse in Texas."

"But you fill a need here. The office isn't the same without you."

"We've had this discussion. I know you like hearing about the cop stuff, but I don't see a lot here to interest me."

Jill looked away. "Let's talk about something else."

"I had a call from Liz. She wants to rent my townhouse."

"Liz mentioned she had an opportunity to get a place of her own. I got the impression her motivation was being out of the Park Service housing and being somewhere she could entertain a male visitor."

I nodded. "She said she had a roommate lined up to split the rent. I didn't pry, but I wonder if it's Jamie."

Jill relaxed and nodded. "That'd be nice. They got along well on the trek. I think they enjoyed each other's company, but they need a little time to feel their way through the development of a relationship."

"They need to overcome their clash of cultures."

We moved on to other topics and Jill laughed at my stories about Federal training. Our plates were cleared, and Jill waved off my attempt to pay the bill. The waiter looked uneasy when he approached our table a few minutes later.

"I'm very sorry, but it's Friday night and we have people waiting for tables. If you're through . . ." We nodded our understanding and waved off his apology.

We walked to the Park Service pickup in silence and Jill started the engine to warm the interior. She looked at me, her expression sad. "The restaurant wasn't the right place for this discussion." She paused, staring out the windshield. "The family of the hikers killed in the flash flood filed a negligence suit against the Park Service. I've been suspended, with pay, pending the outcome of the lawsuit."

I played dumb, not wanting to see Brad busted for leaking that information to me. "When did you find out?"

"I got a call on the drive back from Shiprock."

"You should fight the suspension."

"I can, but it'll be in my file and fighting it will just label me as a malcontent. I might be able to force them to reinstate me here, but no one will ever hire me for any other Park Service superintendent job. On top of that, I lost three campers. I received a letter of reprimand citing incompetence for not watching the weather and not being prepared for the possibility of a flash flood." Her eyes glistened with tears.

I twisted to face her. "You're not my boss anymore."

She shook her head. "No, I'm not."

I leaned over and kissed her. She didn't seem surprised, but didn't react, neither resisting nor encouraging me. "If I've misread this, you can slap my face or tell me to get out of the truck."

She took my hand in hers and closed her eyes. I watched a tear trickle down her cheek and wondered if I'd taken advantage of her with all the things that had just come crashing down. I expected to be walking home.

She leaned across the seat and pressed her lips against mine tenderly. I pulled her close and slipped my tongue between her lips. I felt her body quiver. She leaned back and wiped the tear away. She pulled a tissue from her pocket and wiped her nose. Then she backed out of the parking spot and pulled onto the road. We drove back to my townhouse in silence.

Jill looked at my neighbor's dark windows. "It looks like Sheila didn't wait up for you."

"I think the boys get up early so she watches the news and goes to bed."

Jill opened the pickup door and stepped out. We walked to my townhouse door in awkward silence.

"Do you want to come in? I could make coffee."

Jill shook her head "You're very special, but I'm too old for one-night stands, and you're on your way to Texas." She walked quickly back to the pickup.

I thought about following, but she'd summed up her situation. I couldn't come up with an argument that didn't sound pathetic or manipulative. I locked the door, threw the keys on the breakfast nook, and put my gun and holster on top of the refrigerator. The previous long days and uncomfortable nights sleeping on the ground had a cumulative effect and I suddenly felt very tired. I took off my hiking boots and left them in front of the couch, then threw my dirty clothes in the hamper as I walked to the shower. The pounding hot water felt heavenly, and I realized I hadn't showered, shaved, or changed clothes before we'd gone to the restaurant. I must've smelled and looked like I'd spent three days on a cattle drive. I let the hot water soak my beard and I shaved off three days of stubble in the shower, finishing as the hot water ran out. I was drying off when my cellphone rang. The Caller ID said JRickowski.

"What's up, Jill?"

"I'm standing outside your front door. I rang the doorbell a couple times, but you didn't answer. Is that a hint?"

I rushed to unlock the door. Jill looked at my wet hair and the towel wrapped around my waist. "Oh, you were in the shower."

"Did you forget something?"

"I waited until I got my courage up." She pulled my head down and our mouths met, kissing hungrily. She closed the door, turned off the kitchen lights, and pulled me toward the hallway.

"What happened to your rule about one-night stands?"

"Shut up before I lose my nerve."

I led her to the bedroom and kissed her as I undid the buttons on her uniform blouse. Before I got to the last button, she pulled me close and we stood hugging, her face buried in my shoulder.

"I could find an old movie on TV and we could just snuggle on the couch." I meant what I was telling her, but my body reacted and I knew she could feel the lump under the towel pressing against her.

She looked up at me and stared into my eyes. "You'd really do that, wouldn't you?"

"If that's what you want. I won't take advantage of you."

She pressed her hips against me. "What I want is to make love to my best friend. I've wanted to do this since before you went away to Federal cop school. But there was the supervisor issue and I didn't want you to think I was using sex as a lever to keep you here. Then I was afraid of getting involved and being hurt." She ran her fingers along my jaw, then touched them to my lips. "Please turn off the lights. I'm going to hop in your shower for just a second."

I turned off the lights and threw back the bedcovers. I dropped the towel next to the bed and slipped between the sheets. I watched her back as she slipped off her blouse and pants. She looked over her shoulder and saw me watching her undress in the moonlight glowing through the bedroom blinds.

"Turn the other way."

I rolled over and a few seconds later I heard the shower running. The shower stopped and the bathroom hinge creaked. The sheet rustled and then I felt the warmth of her damp body pressed against my back.

"I guess you're not accustomed to female visitors."

"What was the giveaway?"

"Only one toothbrush, manly deodorant, manly shampoo, and no conditioner. My hair is going to look like a scarecrow tomorrow."

"There hasn't been a woman in this bathroom since I moved in. You might find some girly things my cousin left in the guest bathroom."

"It's been a long time since I've shared a bed." Her arms wrapped around me and she ran her fingers through the hair on my chest. "My fiancé was a cowboy and he acted the same with me or a bronco. It was all about him. I was just his plaything."

I rolled over, cupped her face in my hand and caressed it. She closed her eyes and let out a small gasp.

"You're so gentle."

I explored the curves of her body with my fingertips. We spent a half hour touching, kissing, then gently coupling. The events of the previous days were erased.

I was nodding off when I heard her whisper, "Doug."

"Yes?"

"Do you think you could . . ." She stopped before completing the question.

"What, Honey?"

"Honey?" I could see her smile in the moonlight.

I kissed her gently.

"Could you be with someone six years older, who's built more like a tomboy than a Playboy model?"

"You're prettier and smarter than any woman in a girlie magazine."

"I appreciate the kind lie." She snuggled into my chest. "But if we got to know each other, could you . . ."

"Shh." I realized that under her tough shell, Jill had been totally messed up by her first romantic experience. For the first time in thirty years she'd let her guard down. I felt overwhelmed she'd chosen me to share herself.

She put her arm across my chest, her leg over my thigh, and her head on my shoulder. When her breathing slowed, I slid her head onto the pillow and adjusted the sheet to cover her shoulders. I kissed her on the top of her head and whispered, "I know you're asleep, so I'll say this now, because I know you won't believe me when you're awake. I love you."

Thoughts of Texas kept me awake despite my overwhelming fatigue.

When I fell asleep, I dreamt of coyotes calling. Jill and I were walking through the high desert where the snow hung from Juniper branches. I held her hand like I never wanted to let it go.

"Ouch!"

I awoke slowly from my dream. "What?"

"You were crushing my hand."

"Sorry. I was dreaming."

"Was your dream about me?" Jill rolled over and tucked her head under my chin.

"Can you take a week off?"

"What?"

"Can you take some time off work?"

"I'm on paid leave pending the outcome of the flash flood investigation."

"I'll buy two tickets to Texas in the morning."

"What are you talking about?"

"You asked if I could be happy with someone a little older and smarter."

"That's not exactly what I said."

"Let's fly to Texas and find out."

"What happens if . . ."

"You said you weren't into one-night stands. Let's spend a week at the San Antonio Riverwalk and see what happens."

"So, we play lovebirds in San Antonio for a few days, then what?" I heard apprehension in her voice.

"My Port Aransas townhouse is only two blocks from the ocean. We can walk the beach holding hands every evening."

I felt her muscles relax. "Is that what you were dreaming about when you were squeezing my hand?"

"I didn't want to let you go."

The End

Dean Hovey is the award-winning author of two mystery series set in Minnesota and the Doug Fletcher mystery series set in Arizona. His travel, scientific background, and research add depth to his characters, plots, and locations. He splits his year between Minnesota and Arizona.

www.ingramcontent.com/pod-product-compliance
Lightning Source LLC
Chambersburg PA
CBHW072359110726
47909CB00003B/749